当代文学名著英译丛书

汉英对照

屋檐水 杨争光诗选

杨争光 著

胡宗锋
[英]罗宾·吉尔班克 译

陕西师范大学出版总社

图书代号：WX19N2010

图书在版编目(CIP)数据

屋檐水：杨争光诗选：汉英对照/杨争光著；胡宗锋，（英）罗宾·吉尔班克译. —西安：陕西师范大学出版总社有限公司，2020.1
ISBN 978-7-5613-9804-3

Ⅰ.①屋… Ⅱ.①杨…②胡…③罗… Ⅲ.①诗集—中国—当代—汉、英 Ⅳ.①I227

中国版本图书馆CIP数据核字（2019）第136652号

屋檐水：杨争光诗选 汉英对照
WUYANSHUI YANGZHENGGUANGSHIXUAN

杨争光 著
胡宗锋 [英]罗宾·吉尔班克 译

选题策划	刘东风
责任编辑	张 佩
责任校对	郭永新 穆语彤
封面设计	白砚川
出版发行	陕西师范大学出版总社
	（西安市长安南路199号 邮编710062）
网　址	http://www.snupg.com
印　刷	西安市建明工贸有限责任公司
开　本	889mm×1194mm 1/32
印　张	8.5
插　页	2
字　数	150千
版　次	2020年1月第1版
印　次	2020年1月第1次印刷
书　号	ISBN 978-7-5613-9804-3
定　价	36.00元

读者购书、书店添货或发现印刷装订问题，请与本公司营销部联系、调换。
电话：（029）85307864 85303629   传真：（029）85303879

目 录
Contents

1980年

002 小马

004 无题

006 老树

1981年

008 嬉戏

012 你许给我一片黎明

016 螺丝钉

018 自由

020 冰凌

024 土地（四首）

034 冬天，一个农民的孩子死了

042 窗外是充实的寒冷

046 给S

048 爱不是倾诉

1982年

050 野鸽子

056 外祖父

070 三棵树

074 妈妈

092 原野

003   Pony

005   Untitled

007   Old Tree

009   Joyful Play

013   You promised me a piece of dawn

017   Screw

019   Liberty

021   Icicles

025   Fields (Four Poems)

035   Winter, a farmer's child has died

043   It is cold enough outside the window

047   For S

049   Love does not mean pouring out your heart

051   Wild Pigeons

057   Maternal grandfather

071   Three Trees

075   Mother

093   Open Plain

1983年

- 094 我站在北京的街道上了
- 106 一位老人和一个孩子
- 108 洗衣服的女人

1984年

- 112 思念
- 118 是秋天了
- 122 歌手
- 124 梅香
- 128 朋友

1985年

- 132 大青马
- 136 这些山
- 140 石板房
- 144 那个汉子……
- 146 老家
- 160 大西北

1986年

- 168 黄土高原（六首）
- 186 牡丹台

095 I stand on the streets of Beijing

107 An Old Man and a Child

109 The washerwoman

113 Longing

119 It is Autumn now

123 Singer

125 Sweet Plum

129 Friends

133 The Big Black Horse

137 These mountains

141 House of Slate

145 That Macho Man

147 Hometown

161 The Great Northwest

169 The Loess Plateau (Six Pieces)

187 Peony Pavilion

198 鼓阵

208 窗花

212 那个人

216 雪花的孩子

218 憩息

1987年

222 屋檐水

1988年

234 交谈：自言自语

2007年

258 落叶

199 Drum Formation

209 Papercut on the window

213 That man

217 Snowflake's Child

219 A Short Break

223 Water from the Eaves

235 Conversation: Talking with One's Self

259 Fallen Leaves

杨争光诗选
Slected Poems of Yang Zhengguang

1980年

小 马

它睡着了
在安详的梦里
捕捉着幻想——

绿色的波浪
绿色的风
绿色的阳光……

如果它知道
有人正挽制笼头
它该有多么悲伤!

Pony

He is sleeping

Capturing illusions

In his peaceful dream

Green waves

Green wind

Green sunshine…

If he knew

Someone was fashioning a harness

How sad he would be

无 题

听不见蝉声
也没有了风

记忆和灯光一起
发酵着血腥

蜘蛛把生活的故事
从墙角织进怅惘的眼睛

钟摆,像槌
枯瘦的心被又一次敲肿

静静的夜
淡淡的星

Untitled

Hearing no chirp of cicadas

No gusting wind either

Memory and lamplight

Leaven bloodied articles

In the corner a spider spins everyday annals

Into eyes filled with melancholy

The hammer-like pendulum

Pummels the thin heart swollen again

Still is the night

And sparse the stars

老　树

乌鸦飞走了
像一颗黑色的流星

失落了梦的灵魂
显得虚空

你把冰冷的手
伸向星星……

Old Tree

The crow whisked away

Like a black meteor

The dream lost its soul

And appears vacant

You stretch out an icy hand

Toward the stars

1981年

嬉 戏

一朵朵浪花飞来
她跳着,追逐着
在采摘。像白蝴蝶
裙子在飘,帆儿
在波浪上轻轻地摇摆

她把一串串洁白的笑
和浪珠兜了一怀

海去了
笑声碎了,像一瓣瓣
粉红色的桃花
不再回来。她
和沙滩一起站着
眼睛里噙满悲哀

Joyful Play

Waves erupt blossom-like, one upon another
She jumps and gives chase
Trying to pluck them. Like a white butterfly
Her skirt floats, and the sail
Sways gently on the waves

She gathers a chest-ful of laughter
And pearly waves

The sea has gone
The laughter is shattered, as
Petals of pink peach blossom
Never to return. She
Stands together with the beach
Eyes full of grief

海在响,在远处
在她蓝色的眼睛里澎湃

The sea is roaring in the distance

Surging and slumping in her blue eyes

你许给我一片黎明

你许给我一片黎明
和玻璃一起镶上窗扇——
它滑走了,像风
像黑暗中的一闪

你许给我自由的帆
我孩子般地扑向海岸——
帆呢?时间的眼泪
敲打着荒凉的沙滩

你许给我羽毛笔管
让我画风,画云
把黑夜画成白天——
我又一次错了,像种子
把爱嫁给了冰川

也许你收回了
当初的诺言
也许这一切

You promised me a piece of dawn

You promised me a piece of dawn
And adorned the pane and I with drapes —
It slid away like the wind
Like a flash in the dark

You promised me a free sail
Childishly I bumped towards the seashore —
Where was the sail? The tears of time
Pounded the desolate strand

You promised me a tube of a quill
To let me limn the wind and clouds
To paint night into day —
I was wrong again, as a seed
That offered its love to an icicle

Perhaps you have rescinded
Your opening promise
Perhaps everything was

本来就是欺骗

我恨
我不能说
只在沉默中划亮火柴
烧红一根廉价的烟卷

Fraudulent from the off

I loathe

Being unable to speak

I can only strike a match in silence

And make a woodbine fizzle red

螺丝钉

一滴干枯的眼泪
一块冻结的热情
我被黑夜利用
不,我不是英雄——

为了狼眼睛似的天空
真正的英雄刚刚死去
黎明的海上
漂着他带血的头颅……

Screw

A dry and withered tear

A shard of frozen passion

I was used by the night

No, I am not a hero —

For the wolf-eyed heavens

The true hero has just perished

On the sea at dawn

His bloodied head bobs …

自　由

农夫冰冷的铁犁
插进温热的泥土
鸟儿用颤动的翅膀
写在遥远的天际

睡莲把浓重的色彩
涂进月光的梦里
战士把殷红的血液
滴在闪光的枪刺

是摆向黄昏的花圈
是响在黎明的婴啼
是生命绷紧的缆绳
是射满弹洞的旗帜

一个古老的童话
一个常新的命题

Liberty

The farmer's ice-cold iron coulter
Is thrust into warm soil
The birds, their wings atremble
Sketch something in the heavens faraway

The pygmy waterlily casts strong hues
Onto the dreams below the moonlight
Warriors shed their red blood
Onto the bayonets on rifles

It is a wreath laid out for the dusk
It is an infant bawling at daybreak
It is a lifeline pulled taut
It is a bullet-perforated banner

An ancient fairytale
A theme perpetually new

冰 凌

1
既然命运已经注定
它没有怨恨冬天
在星星睡去的时候
一队赤条条的孩子
把洁白的幻想
挨个儿挂满屋檐

2
仿佛来自遥远的世纪
珍珠的声音
敲打死去的记忆,敲打着
最后一个寒冷的日子
就这样,它哭了
一滴一滴
暖热了土地
呼唤起紫云英、星星草
甚至蒺藜

Icicles

1

Since fate already predetermined

It would not bellyache about winter

When the stars went to sleep

A group of stark naked kids

Dangled their pure white illusions

Upon the eaves in a row

2

They seemed to have come from a faraway century

The sound of the pearls

Pounded at the dead memory, pounded at

The last cold day

In this way it wept

Drop by drop

It warmed the soil

Awakened the milk vetch, the star grass

一个绿色的家族
从地平线上云一样涌起
一片片手掌上
跳跃着一万个太阳
于是,这苦难的队伍
向无云的天空
开始远征

3
在它死去的那刻
遥远的天边——
海在响

And even the puncture vine

A verdant family clan

Rushing up from the horizon like a cloud

Upon the palms

Ten thousand suns jumped

So, this troop formed of hardship

Commenced their long march

Towards the cloudless sky

3

That moment it died

At the far ends of the earth—

The sea was roaring

土地（四首）

父 亲

他睡了，在凸凹不平的田埂上睡了
野风掀开他被汗水泡硬的布衫
向太阳坦露着结实的胸肌
拥挤的肋骨整齐地排列成岩石的队伍
他睡了，锄头弯曲在禾苗的背后
他睡了，牛一样地喘着粗气
起伏的胸膛缩小和放大着天空
手臂在延伸，脚趾在无拘无束地生长

他睡了，脊背压平了石头和土块
压平了野草和蝈蝈的叫声
一切都已消失，一切都已忘记
没有过黄昏，没有过早晨
没有过祖先被风雨泡涨的故事
树一样，又移植在他的梦里
无数条河流曾漫过他宽阔的额头
留下曲线，留下道路，留下生命的象形文字

Fields (Four Poems)

Father

He slept, on the undulating terrain of the field

The wild wind fanned ajar his sweat-soaked shirt

His sturdy chest being exposed to the sun

The pinched ribs fell into line like a platoon of rocks

He slept, as the hoe curved behind the seedlings

He slept, breathing thickly as a bull

His pulsing chest expanded then constricted the heavens

His arms stretched, his toes grew without restraint

He slept, his back slapped the stones and earth flat

Levelling the chirps of wild grass and grasshoppers

Everything vanished, everything was forgotten

There was no dusk, no morning

No annals of his wind and rain-drenched ancestors

Transplanted tree — like into his dreams

Countless rivers once inundated his broad brow

Leaving curves, paths, and pictographs of life

没有过冬天，没有过炎热

没有过孩子饥饿时的眼睛和妻子无力的啜泣

大片的庄稼曾在他粗糙的手掌上一次次成熟

收割，又一次次潮水般涌起

留下坚硬的老茧，留下层层叠叠的山脉

长满不能收获、不会倒伏的荆棘

他睡了，狗一样地睡了

一切都已消失，一切都已忘记

只有笨重的呼吸和脊背一同起伏

把土地给他的疲劳又交还给土地

头顶的太阳集合起一万道强光

把慈祥和幸福赠给他熟睡的躯体

赠给永恒，赠给一个雕满苦难的纪念碑

戴草帽的姑娘

她沿着长长的田埂走过来了

戴着一顶草帽走过来了

脸上扑满太阳的颜色

像田野上霞光一样张开的小路

像夏天的庄稼一样摇动的波浪

粗糙的布衫上

There was no winter and no balmy summer

Nor the eyes of ravenous kids and the weep of a helpless wife

Large swathes of crops ripened on his coarse palms

And were harvested, they surged again and again like waves

Leaving hard calluses and layers and layers of mountains

Full of thorns which would neither fall nor be reaped

He slept, like a hound

Everything vanished, all was forgotten

Only his heavy breath and back rose and fell in unison

He returned the fatigue to the fields that had given him it

The sun overhead harnessed the power of ten thousand beams

Offering kindness and mirth to his sound asleep frame

Offering them to eternity and a statue wrought through hardship

The Girl in a Straw Hat

She walked over the field's long, long terrain

Wearing a straw hat

Her face draped in the colour of sunshine

A small path opening its mouth like the sunglow the fields

Like crops swaying in the summer waves

On her coarse cotton blouse

流动着风的线条

卷起的裤腿沾满金色的泥巴

好看的脚丫踏醒青草的芬芳

少女的梦从这里开始动荡了

少女的胸脯从这里开始起伏了

像微黄的苹果树一样不安而优美

像五月的天空一样健康而开朗

她走过来了,走过来了

带着大平原粗犷的气息

带着头发一样潮湿的早晨

走向庄稼,走向汗水和疲倦

走向秋天,走向快乐和成熟

割麦子的母亲和捡麦穗的小女孩

她笑了,摇着乱蓬蓬的小脑袋

对着正在收割的母亲笑了

黑色的眼睛葡萄一样清甜

小篮儿在飘,小辫儿在飘

像一株未成熟的麦穗摇向天边

忧伤的目光在田野上滑落了

忧伤的目光从田野里长出来了——

Flowed the strains of the wind

Her rolled-up trousers stained with golden mud

Her elegant toes awakened the fragrance of green grass

The dream of a maiden started swaying from here

The breast of the maiden started to heave and fall from here

Restless and beautiful like pale yellow apple tree

Hale and optimistic like a May sky

She walked over, she walked over

With the rough breath of the big plain

With the morning dew moist like her hair

Walking towards the crops, sweat and fatigue

Walking towards the autumn, happiness and maturity

The Mother Reaper and the Girl Gleaner

She smiled, and shook her small, mussy head

Beaming at her reaping mother

Her dark eyes sweet as grapes

Her little basket hovering, her little pigtail hovering

Pointing skyward like an unripe ear of wheat

That sorrowful gaze slid down onto the field

That sorrowful gaze sprouted up from the field—

小篮儿在飘,小辫儿在飘
正在衰老的母亲想起她

一幅丢失了年代的画……

哺乳的母亲
土坎上,一位少妇
正在给孩子哺乳
她是从庄稼地里走来的
她是从绿色的波涛中走来的
头发上的玉米叶
像一缕飘动的风
她是母亲,她不会羞涩
像秋天抱起一个鲜艳的苹果
捧给早晨的太阳
她半袒着美丽的胸膛
把鼓胀的乳房
捧给孩子
眼睛里布满慈祥
母亲衰老了,她没有衰老
在同一个土坎上
母亲曾哺乳过她

Her little basket hovering, her little pigtail hovering

The ageing mother recalled her past

A painting forgets its date of origin …

A suckling mother

On the earthy terrain, a young lady

Is feeding her baby with her breast

She walks out from the fields of crops

She walks out from the waves of green

Sweet-corn leaves upon her hair

Like a gust of floating wind

She is the mother, not at all shy

Like autumn holding up a bright apple

Offering it to the morning sun

She half-exposes her fine bust

Offering her swelling breasts

To the kid

Her eyes filled with kindness

The mother is growing old, but she is not

On this same earthy terrain

Her mother fed her as well

用乳汁延长了自己

她也会衰老
她给她的孩子哺乳了
把自己延长给又一个崭新的躯体
延长着劳动，延长着精力
延长着庄稼一次又一次收割
土地永远年轻的秘密

现在，怀中的孩子满足地笑了
她扣好纽扣
她拉住衣襟
理一理蓬乱的头发
又走进田野
用汗水去喂养土地

And prolonged her life with her breast milk

She will grow old
Prolonging herself through another new body
Prolonging labour, prolonging vitality
Prolonging the secret of the crops
Which have been harvested again and again
And the land that is forever young

Now, the kid at her bosom with smiles contentedly
She buttons up
her garments
Combs her mussy hair
Walks into the fields of crops again
And feeds the land with her sweat

冬天，一个农民的孩子死了

蓝眼睛的小花猫听不见她低低的歌声了
田野里的风不能抚摸她乱蓬蓬的黑头发了
路边的青草不能用露水打湿她穿着布鞋的脚了
弯弯的小溪流不能照着她背着书包走过小桥了
洁白的雪花第八次悄悄地落了
迟落的雪花不能第八次吻她红红的脸蛋了

冬天，一个农民的孩子死了

她是一个忧郁的孩子
她爱坐在门槛上数天上的星星
她还不知道云儿为什么不是一只小船
驮她到书上见过的那一座美丽的小岛
她也不知道雪花为什么不是蓝的
就像她睡梦中点亮的那盏蓝色的灯笼
在田野上拾柴禾的时候
她总要摘下一朵蒲公英，让风儿
从小手心里轻轻地吹上高空
洁白的羽毛带着她的心事飞走了

Winter, a farmer's child has died

The blue-eyed little piebald kitten cannot hear her low singing
The breeze of the fields cannot stroke her unruly black hair
The green grass on the roadside cannot bedew her cloth-shoed feet
The curving brooks cannot reflect her with her satchel on the bridge
The pure snowflakes fell silently for the eighth time
The belated snowflake could not kiss her red face for the eighth time

Winter, a farmer's child has died

She was a melancholy mite
She was fond of perching on the threshold, counting stars
She didn't know why each cloud was not a gondola
Which would carry her to the beautiful island in her book
She didn't know why the snowflake wasn't blue
Like the blue lantern she lit in her dreams
While gathering firewood in the fields
She would always pluck a dandelion, and let the wind
Puff the clocks up gently from her little palm
Pure white feathers gliding away with the load from her mind

她的眼睛像初夏的早晨一样潮湿……

冬天,一个农民的孩子死了

她不能给背着圆圆的太阳锄地的爸爸送茶水了
也不能和爸爸拉着地板车上县城的大街卖菠菜了
她不能给劳累的妈妈唱那支刚刚学会的歌儿了
也不能在妈妈生病时踮起脚尖上锅台做饭了
她不能咬着铅笔杆想那道神秘的算术题了
也不能给犁田回来的老牛擦脖子上的热汗了

冬天,一个农民的孩子死了

她是一个细心的孩子
她总爱躲在一个地方学妈妈洗衣服的样子
在木板上揉着找来的布条,歪着头
把甜甜的微笑紧紧地抿在嘴唇里
蓬乱的头发滑落了,她好看地扬向鬓角
伸伸胳膊,像妈妈那样呼一口长气
她还做了一个穿着花布衫的布娃娃
一个人的时候,她就美好地抱着它
给它"喂奶",拍着它悄悄地睡进梦里
她是女孩子,她也要做母亲啊

Her eyes were as moist as the early summer morning ...

Winter, a farmer's child has died

No more could she send tea for her dad who hoed with the round sun on his back
No more could she pull the spinach cart with her dad to the market
No more could she rouse her shattered ma with freshly-learned lyrics
No more could she tiptoe around the kitchen as her substitute when ill
No more could she munch her pencil and cogitate over mysterious equations
No more could she wipe away the cows sweat after ploughing

Winter, a farmer's child has died

She was an attentive girl
Fond of hiding in some corner, imitating her mother doing the laundry
With her head tilted, she would rub strips of cloth she found on a board
Tucking back the sweet grin on her lips
Delicately she combed up the unruly hair which slid down
She stretched her arms and sighed like her mother

冬天,一个农民的孩子死了

她得的是乡下的一种常见的病
她死在通往县城医院的路上了
十二里地,她没有跨过死亡的门槛
她死在一个寒冷的冬天里了

她见过的小鸟们仍在树枝上唱着歌儿
她采过的野花仍在一次又一次美丽地开放
庄稼地里的人仍在默默地劳动
遥远的城市,工人们仍在上班和下班

冬天,一个农民的孩子死了

她安静地躺在土地里了
和那个喂牛的老汉躺在一起了
雪花在一片一片地凋落
落在弯弯的小路上了
落在一个小小的坟堆上了

所有描写女人的书都是为她而作的
所有描写母亲的书都是为她而作的

She too had fashioned a doll wearing flowery clothes
When alone, she would caress her kindly
"Suckling" her, she patted her quietly into dreams
She was a girl who also wanted to be a mother

Winter, a farmer's child has died

She contracted a typical country disease
And died en route to the county clinic
Twelve itdicise still to go, she couldn't out-leap death's threshold
She passed on in a cold winter

The little birds she had spied were still chirping on the boughs
The wildflowers she had picked were again in merry full bloom
The folks in the field still laboured silently
vIn the cities faraway, workers still clocked on and off

Winter, a farmer's child has died

She lay on the earth at peace
Together with the old cattle hand
Snowflakes descended one-by-one
folling onto the curving path

所有描写爱的书都是为她而作的
所有描写悲哀的书都是为她而作的啊

冬天,一个农民的孩子死了

folling onto the tiny grave mound

All the books describing women were composed for her

All the books describing motherhood were composed for her

All the books describing love were composed for her

All the books describing sorrow were composed for her

Winter, a farmer's child has died

窗外是充实的寒冷

窗外是充实的寒冷
窗里是充实的温暖
温暖居住在寒冷里面
我憋不住了
一把扯开门帘
把一行不冷静的脚印
种在冷静的白雪上面
还记得吗
那个寂寞的日子
我们在一起
凋落的雪花正在沉淀
你解开那条鲜艳的围巾
在结满冰花的小树上
点起一团飘动的火焰

是调和，还是挑战？
你把冻红的手指放在唇边
你没有颤抖，你说了
说是为了心里的一幅画

It is cold enough outside the window

It is cold enough outside the window

It is warm enough inside

The warmth resides within the coldness

I cannot tolerate this

I push the door curtain open

Plant a line of ludicrous footprints

On the sober-minded snow

Still remembering

Those lonely days

When we were together

The waning snowflakes settled

You untied that gaily-coloured scarf

Lit up a floating fire

On the icicle-bound saplings

Harmonious or challenging

You touched your lips with cold-reddened fingers

You didn't shiver, you said

This was for a painting in your heart

已画了几个冬天

很远很远了

还能看见……

Being composed over several winters

It has gone further and further

But can still be seen ...

给S

我画了一只受了伤的小鹿
悲哀地望着林中的小路
你说它一定想妈妈了
很远的地方,有一间青藤小屋

你默默地把画儿移上窗台
让阳光在小路上慢慢地流
望着你噙满泪珠的眼睛
我想说很多话,一句也没有说出

For S

I drew a wounded little hind

Which scanned the forest paths in sorrow

You said it must be thinking of its ma

In a faraway place, stood a hut woven from vines

Silently you moved the painting to the windowsill

Let the sunshine ooze slowly along those paths

Watching your eyes full of tears

I was mute, though I had so much to say

爱不是倾诉

想让你的眼睛不再是朦胧的湖
想让你的头发不再是飘浮的雾
想把你窗口的灯光挂上小船
我就是河流
用我的手臂托着你向天涯摆渡
有星星就有露珠
在清晨和午夜相遇
爱不是倾诉
是没有索取的给予
爱不是倾诉
是一颗心在另一颗心里
平安地居住

Love does not mean pouring out your heart

I want your eyes to no longer be an obscure lake

I want your hair to no longer be a floating fog

I want to hang the lamp from your window on a small boat

I am a river

Holding you in my arms, I shall ferry you to the ends of the earth

If there are stars there will be dewdrops

Meeting in the morning and at midnight

Love does not mean pouring out your heart

It is offering without taking

Love does not mean pouring out your heart

It is one heart living within another

Peacefully

1982年

野鸽子

1
当黎明和风在上升的陆地上
剪出一棵棵云杉的时候
野鸽子呢

当冬天在年老的树上
摇落一片片洁白的羽毛的时候
野鸽子呢

她在太阳金色的脊背上
她在结满冰花的窗台上
冬天有多么孤寂
她有多么孤寂

Wild Pigeons

1

When dawn and wind snip out spruce trees one-by-one

On the rising continent

What about the wild pigeons

When winter shakes away

Pure white feathers from ancient trees

What about the wild pigeons

She rode on the golden back of the sunshine

She rode on the windowsill full of icicles

As forlorn as the lonely winter was

Forlorn and lonely was she

2
飘雪的时候
野鸽子在很远的地方唱歌
她为她的歌声感动了

她没有抖落苦难
她用羸弱的翅膀承受着苦难
她没有诅咒寒冷
她用诚实的眼睛注视着寒冷
另一个遥远的地方
雪花撩拨着窗帘
门为冬天打开了
雪地上升起洁白的回声

飘雪的时候
野鸽子在很远的地方唱歌
冬天有多么辽阔
她有多么辽阔

3
她起飞了

2

When snow floated

Wild pigeons cooed in a distant place

She was moved by the singing

She didn't shake off suffering

She bore it with her weak pinions

She didn't curse the cold

She gazed at it with honest eyes

In another distant place

The snowflakes teased the window curtain

The door was open for winter

A pure white echo rose from in the snowy land

When the snow was floating

The wild pigeons sang in a distant place

As broad and as vast as the winter was

Broad and vast was she

3

She took flight

衔着为冬天创造的歌声
冬天有多么严峻
她有多么严峻

With the song she created for winter on her beak

As stern as the winter was

Stern was she

外祖父

1
鸟儿的歌声飘在土槐树的叶子上
土槐树的叶子飘在稻草屋上
稻草屋里有一个诚实的土炕
诚实的土炕温暖着外祖父常年的梦想

2
年轻的时候
外祖父给典狱长背过枪
典狱长的丫鬟是他的妻子
可怜的丫鬟不会生育
外祖父学会了悲伤

当渭河在秋天里又一次涨水的时候
河水卷走了无数个村庄
那是一个美好的早晨
太阳升起的地方

Maternal grandfather

1

The birdsong floated on the leaves of the Chinese scholar tree
The leaves of the scholar tree floated over the roof of the straw hut
There was an honest itdice in that hut
It warmed the yearly dreams of the maternal grandfather

2

When he was young
He carried the rifle for the prison governor
The governor's maid being his bride
That pitiful maid was barren
Grandpa learned the meaning of sorrow

When the River Wei overflowed again in autumn
The floodwater swept away villages without number
That was one exquisite morning
In the place where the sun rose

漂来一只木盆
木盆里坐着一个婴儿
她是我的妈妈
妈妈的哭声揪住了外祖父的心

外祖母死去的时候
妈妈长大了
妈妈出嫁的时候
外祖父老了
他默默地走进县城
买回来两只绵羊

那是两只可爱的绵羊啊
长长的犄角就像晚上弯弯的月亮
他常坐在门口的石头上看它们吃草
像和忠实的朋友一起
享受着同一个美好的时光

3
我是在乡下长大的
小窝里下蛋的老母鸡是我的朋友
土槐树上的麻雀儿是我的朋友

A wooden basin floated over

Propped inside a baby

That was my mother

Her sobs seized the heart of my grandpa

When my maternal grandma died

My mother was grown up

When my mother was married

My maternal grandpa was old

He went to the county town in silence

And bought two sheep

They were indeed lovely

Their long horns curved like the crescent moon of the evening

He would always watch them graze from the rug by the door

Like staying with some bosom friends

He shared the same beautiful time with them

3

I grew up in the countryside

The old hen laying eggs in the coop was my companion

The sparrows on the Chinese scholar tree were my mates

外祖父是我的朋友

飘雪的时候
我和外祖父走进黄昏
捡来的干牛粪点起来了
照亮了外祖父脸上温和的皱纹
我快要蒙眬地睡去了
小树林远远地看着我们
没有一点声响

田野上的黄昏很大很大
黄昏里的我们很小

4
清明节
外祖父领我去上坟
在一个瘦小的坟堆下
睡着我的外祖母

当煤油灯用豆大的光亮在墙壁上
摇晃着我们的身影时
外祖父就给我讲那个遥远的故事

My maternal grandpa was my friend

When the snow floated

I would walk with him into the dusk

Light up the dried cowpats we collected

The fire illuminated the kind wrinkles on his face

I was vaguely about to go to sleep

The small forest peeped at us from afar

Without any sound

The dusk on the fields spread vastly

We were miniscule in the dusk

4

During Tomb-sweeping Festival

Maternal grandpa led me out to sweep

My grandma slept

Beneath a small funerary mound

When the paraffin lamp shone its bean-like light onto the wall

And jostled our shadows about

Grandpa would tell me tales from long ago

他说外祖母很漂亮
就像路边常开的马兰花一样
他说外祖母也是他的朋友
给他做饭，补衣裳
也和他说话，每一句话
都像吃着烧熟的土豆
又热，又香

我不知道外祖母会不会爱我
让我也做她的朋友
外祖父摸着我的头发
他说会的，因为我爱她，想她
想别人的人也不会被别人遗忘

我相信外祖母也是个好人
我把一朵马兰花
插在了那座小坟上

5
我爱田野
我爱在田野上的草丛里捉蚂蚱
外祖父爱田野

He said grandma was very fine

As pretty as the iris blooming on the roadside

He said grandma was his pal

She cooked and made him clothes

Chatted with him, her every word

Being like savouring a baked potato

Warm-tasting, tasting delectable

I don't whether grandma would have loved me or not

And would have befriended me also

Grandpa stroked my hair

And said she would, because I loved and missed her

Someone who misses others will not be forgotten by them

I thought grandma was a fine woman too

I plucked an iris

From the small funerary mound

5

I adored the meadows

I loved to capture grasshoppers among the verdure of the mead

Grandpa loved meadows

他爱在田野上种庄稼
也爱在田野上睡觉
无忧无虑地,就像
他给我讲过的那个远古的皇帝
庄稼是一队队跳舞的宫女
往来的风吹着祝福的叶笛

我睡觉的时候常常做梦
梦见和妈妈在一起
我问外祖父也梦见他的妈妈吗
他总是笑眯眯地看我
我不明白,他为什么还说我
是个傻孩子

6
我上学了
我唱歌儿了
我最爱唱的歌儿
是外祖父教给我的

外祖父会唱的歌儿很多很多
他说他的歌儿都是听来的

He was fond of growing crops there

He was also fond of sleeping there

Without any worries, like

The ancient emperor he told me how

The crops were rows of dancing ladies-in-waiting

The passing breeze blew the flute of blessings

I always have dreams in my sleep

Dreaming of being together with my ma

I asked grandpa if he dreamed of his ma

He would always look at me with a smile

I didn't understand, why he still said that

I was a silly child

6

I began school

I learned to sing

My favourite song

Was the one grandpa taught me

Grandpa knew many

He told me he had heard them from others

春天里唱的，是苦菜花教给他的
夏天里唱的，是苜蓿花教给他的
秋天里唱的，是青蛙教给他的
冬天里唱的，是麦苗在被窝里
悄悄儿给他唱的……

我真羡慕外祖父的耳朵
苦菜花开的时候
我偷偷地坐在花儿的身边
为什么就听不到呢

7

妈妈来了
外祖父病了
外祖父躺在土炕上
妈妈坐在炕沿上
外祖父的脸像土槐树上飘落的叶子
外祖父的眼睛像晒干的庄稼地

外祖父答应我的兔窝还没有盖呀
外祖父答应我的小白兔还没有买呀
外祖父不再笑了

The songs of spring, were taught to him by bitter herbs

The songs of summer, were taught to him by alfalfa

The songs of autumn, were taught to him by frogs

The songs of winter, were sung secretly to him

By wheat shoots beneath quilts ...

I really admired grandpa's ear

When the bitter herbs were in bloom

I sat by them covertly

Why could I hear nothing

7

My mother dropped by

My grandpa was ill

He was lying on the kang

My mother perched on the edge

Grandpa's face was like the floating leaves of the scholar tree

Grandpa's eyes were like dried fields of crops

Grandpa hadn't built the rabbit hutch that he promised me

Grandpa hadn't bought the white bunny he promised me

Grandpa didn't smile any more

不和我说话了
妈妈说外祖父要和她谈大人们的事情
她赶我到学校去念书

妈妈,外祖父是我的朋友啊
我知道外祖父爱我
你为什么那么霸道呢

8
外祖父死了
妈妈说他找外祖母去了
我坐在外祖父的坟堆旁
我没哭,我不回去
我在看坟堆旁的那丛毛毛草
我在看远处的那片小树林
我相信快要下雪了
干牛粪又会点起来的
我和外祖父坐在黄昏里
他在唱那支低低的歌谣……

Nor did he speak to me

Mother said he had some adult things to say to her

She drove me to school to read

Mother, I was grandpa's friend

I knew he loved me very much

Why be so high-handed

8

Grandpa died

Mother told me he had gone to look for grandma

I sat beside his funerary mound

I didn't cry, I didn't want to go back

I was looking at the heap of grass beside the mound

I was looking at the small forest in the distance

I believed that snow was coming soon

Dry cowpats would be lit again

Grandpa and I would sit in the dusk

In a low voice he would sing that solo ballad …

三棵树

寒流曾呼啸着从头顶滚过
抽动的枝条和黎明一起振响
在激动中画出疯狂的曲线
围绕着太阳
夜来时,声音在沉淀
三个并排的冷静
在原野上
守卫着宇宙的寂寞

当冬天摘去最后一片叫喊的叶子
它们拥抱着死了
对看天空,没有诅咒
也不再战栗
枝丫交错着,只把搏斗的形象
固定在这里
像冻结在土地的胸膛上
一行古老的文字
一条条不死的道路
从这里伸向遥远

Three Trees

A cold stream roars over their tops

The shivering boughs vibrate with the dawn

And draw a ludic curve in excitement

Encircling the sun

In the night, the sound is sinking

The sober-minded trio stand in a row

On the field

Guarding the loneliness of the cosmos

When the winter has picked off the last of the shouting leaves

They will embrace one another and die together

Facing the sky, they refrain from cursing

With their boughs intertwined, they only leave

The frozen image of their struggle

Like a line of ancient characters

Frozen on the chest of the earth

Rows of never-dying paths

Stretch afar from here

又从遥远处

向这里汇集

Then from afar

They gather here again

妈 妈

1
我家在渭河平原上
妈妈是在平原上长大的

土地上的扒地草拖蔓蔓了
妈妈扎小辫儿了
田野上的荞麦花开过六次了
妈妈挎上挖野菜的小竹篮了
当荞麦第十二次开花的时候
妈妈摇着纺车纺线了
嗡嗡的纺车和扯不完的线儿一起
在圆圆的太阳和圆圆的月亮下
纺着一个女孩子的故事

2
茅草屋的旁边有一棵香椿树
香椿树的叶子伸过纸糊的窗扇了
麻雀儿在香椿树的枝丫上垒窝了

Mother

1

My home was on the Wei River Plain

My mother grew up there

The crawling grass stretched out new suckers

My mother wore her small pigtail

The buckwheat her blossomed six times

Mother picked up her basket for digging wild greens

When the buckwheat blossomed for the twelfth time

Mother assembled the spinning wheel

The din of the wheel and the endless thread

Span the story of a girl

Under the round sun and moon

2

There was a toon tree alongside the grass-thatched hut

When its leaves stretched over the paper-covered window

And sparrows had woven a nest in its boughs

妈妈出嫁了

她离开了那座熟悉的茅草屋
她没有离开大平原
大平原上的风仍吹着她的头发
大平原上的庄稼仍养育着她

她离开了那棵高高的香椿树
她没有离开纺车儿
在另一个温暖而陌生的土炕沿
纺车儿仍和她说着心里的话

她把长长的发辫儿挽在头上了
她和一个过去不认识的男人一起过活了
人们不再喊她的名字
都叫她"二狗媳妇"了
当我的啼哭跌进那个瓦盆的时候
她又变成"牛牛他妈"了

3
妈妈爱姐姐
她说姐姐长大了能帮她纺线
妈妈爱我

Mother got wed

She quit that familiar grass-thatched hut
But not the plain itself
The breeze of the great plain still stroked her hair
The crops of the great plain were still her sustenance

She may have left that tall toon tree
But not her spinning wheel
She still relayed to it the words upon her mind

She rolled up her long pigtails, pinning them to her head
She went to cohabit with a man she'd never known before
People no more addressed her by her own name
They just called her "Second Dog's wife"
When I was plopped crying into the earthenware basin
They called her "Niu Niu's ma"

3

My mother loved my sister
And said she would help her spin when she was older
My mother loved me

她说我长大了能念书做官
妈妈也爱爸爸
她说爸爸养活着我们一家

冬天,土炕上最热的地方
是我和姐姐的
饭时,小桌上撒落的馍花儿
是妈妈的
当蟋蟀在窗外给星星唱小曲儿时
妈妈用蓬乱的头发挡住灯光
给爸爸缝补着那件
还会被风撕破的衣裳

风雨来了
树上的老鸟伸开宽大的翅膀
护卫着窝里的小鸟
我不明白,妈妈为什么
望着风雨中那只安详的老鸟
要喃喃地说——
"它也是做妈的啊……"

4
妈妈爱钱了

And said, I might go to school and grow up to be an official
My mother loved my father
And declared him the breadwinner

In winter, the warmest part of the italics
Belonger my sister and I
At mealtimes, the pieces of bun which fell off the table
Were all courtesy of my mother
My mother sewed my father's clothes
Which would again be torn open by the wind

When the winds and rain came
The oldbird on the tree would spread its wings wide open
To protect the litlle bird in the nest
I don't know why mother
Peered at the calm old bird in the wind and rain
And murmured —
"She is a mother too …"

4

My mother loved money
She fastened it about her midrib

她的钱是拴在肠子上的
妈妈说钱好
钱能买布、买醋、买盐
她总拍着我的头
说娃娃家不懂得大人的艰难

她很爱她的老母鸡
柜底下放着一个瓦罐
她每天都要数一数里边的鸡蛋
数一次脸上就多一条笑纹
她说等我念书的时候
就用它给我换一件学生蓝
她还说庄户人的日子就要这么过的
一把禾苗,一把粮食,一件布衫……

5
妈妈从省城里回来了
姑婆家住在省城
姑婆的孩子结婚了
妈妈是给姑婆家缝新棉被去的
妈妈是吃表叔的喜酒去的
回来就坐在炕沿上

She said money was good

It can be exchanged for cloth, vinegar, and salt

She always patted my head

And said kids don't know what hardships adults endure

My ma loved her old hen

A pottery jar was stashed beneath the cupboard

Every day she would count the eggs inside

When she counted one further time a smile would wrinkle on her face

She said when I was old enough to go to school

She would trade them for a blue uniform

She said that was how farmers dealt with their live

Seedlings by the bundle, a fistful of grain, cloth in patches ...

5

Mother returned from the provincial city

Where great-auntie lived

Her child had gotten married

My mother went to sew them new cotton quilts

She went there to share my uncle's wedding party

On returning she sat on the edge of the itdics

Telling us tales about city life

给我们讲城里的故事

她说城里人花钱厉害
一顿饭的菜
就够我们家吃一个月的
她说她看不惯他们
不盖房，也不种地
不像过正经日子的样子
她还说城里的人不知道害臊
大白天在街上
男人和女人就挽着胳膊——
乡下的娃娃不能到城里去
去了，会学坏的

不过，她说她羡慕城里人
不愁吃的，不愁穿的
用推娃娃的小车儿，一会儿
就推回来一个月的粮食

好长时间了
皂角树下，庄稼地里
人们还谈论着妈妈
说"牛牛他妈真了不起"

She said that city folks spent cash like water

One meal cost

Our family's monthly allowance

She said she could not bear it

They neither built houses nor ploughed fields

That's not the way to lead a serious life

She said the citizens were without shame

On the streets in broad daylight

Men linked arms with women —

Country kids should not go there

Otherwise they'd be corrupted

However, she added that she admired them

They had cause to worry about food and clothing

Pushing an infant's pram

They could come home with a month's supplies

For a long time

Under the honey locust tree, among the crops

People chattered about my ma

Proclaiming, "Niu Niu's ma was really great"

Proclaiming, "Niu Niu's ma went to the big smoke"

说"牛牛他妈到过城里"

6
爸爸病了
爸爸的病害在肝上
妈妈也病了
妈妈的病害在"愁"上
妈妈说庄稼人
能经得起苦
能出得起力
庄稼人害不起病

爸爸死了
埋在那条弯弯的小路尽头了
留下了姐姐、妹妹和我
留下了黄昏里妈妈长长的哭声
她在哭一个女人的伤心
她在哭一个妻子的不幸
她哭着说她的命不好

大平原上的夜悄悄地落下来了
大平原上的灯一盏一盏的灭了

6

Father was ill

Father had a liver condition

Mother was ill too

Mother had a "worrying" condition

Mother said farmers

Could afford to suffer

Could afford to work hard

But couldn't afford to be ill

Father passed away

Interred at the end of the crooked path

Leaving my elder sister, younger sister and me

Leaving my mother wailing interminably amid the dust

She wailed for the broken heart of a woman

She wailed for the misfortune of a wife

She wailed for the poverty of her fate

Silent fell the night on the great plain

One by one the lamps were extinguished

Only a solitary light was reflected through the window paper

Until daybreak came

有一盏孤独的灯映着窗纸
一直亮到了天明

7
我们的田野里也有一片荞麦地
荞麦年年开花
我家门口也有一棵香椿树
香椿树年年发芽
荞麦花和姐姐的脸蛋一样好看
香椿树和姐姐同年
当荞麦花又一次开放的时候
当香椿树又一次长高的时候
姐姐不念书了

是妈妈不让她念了
妈妈说她是女孩子
庄稼人的女娃能认得工分就行了
庄稼人的女娃要学针线
妈妈说她还没念过书呢
妈妈用她的经验教导着姐姐
妈妈说长大了就要懂事

7

Our fields contained a patch of buckwheat

It blossomed every year

A toon tree stood before our home

The same age as my elder sister

When the buckwheat was in flower again

When the toon tree had grown tall again

My elder sister quit school

Mother was the one who made her do it

Mother said she was a girl

As a farm girl she only needed to read her work points

A farm girl should learn needlepoint

Mother said she herself had no schooling

She could only teach my sis from experience

Mother said girls should grow up to have consideration

My elder sister chewed the end of her pigtail in silence

While crying her eyes red

However, she was obedient

How wretched it was for her

姐姐咬着辫梢儿不说话了
姐姐把眼睛哭红了
可是，姐姐顺从了

姐姐多可怜啊
妈妈多狠心啊
妈妈，我不是恨你
我是恨河滩上的那丛野枣刺

姐姐劳动了
大平原的田野里多了一个戴草帽的姑娘
姐姐纺线了
圆圆的太阳和圆圆的月亮下
嗡嗡的纺车和扯不完的线儿一起
纺着又一个女孩子的故事

8
荞麦又一次开花了

姐姐有婆家了
香椿树又一次长高了
姐姐出嫁了

How hardhearted was my mother

I hated the wild date thorns on the riverbank

My elder sister started labouring

One more girl with a straw hat appeared of the great plain

My sister started to spin a wheel

Under the round sun and moon

The rhythm of the spinning wheel and its endless thread

Span the story of another girl

8

Buckwheat blossomed again

My elder sister gained in-laws

The toon tree grew some more

And she was wed

Like my mother

She didn't leave the great plain

She just switched to working in another field

She just switched to another itdics to spin

和妈妈一样

她没有离开大平原

她只是到另一片庄稼地里劳动去了

她只是到另一个土炕上纺线去了

姐姐出嫁的那天

妈妈老了

当她想姐姐的时候

眼眶里就涌满泪花

姐姐也生儿育女了

姐姐也当妈妈了

当她抱着她的小英英来看我们的时候

我们的妈妈笑了

她说小英英的名字起得文明多了

我不知道姐姐家有没有香椿树

也不知道那里的人

把姐姐叫不叫"英英她妈"

On my elder sister's wedding day

My mother was old

Thinking of my sister

Tears overwhelmed her eyes

My sister also bore children

Becoming a mother herself

When she visited us with little Yingying

Our mother smiled

She said little Yingying's name was very civilised

I don't know if my sister's household had a toon tree of its own

I don't know if the folk over there

Call my sister "Yingying's ma"

原　野

穿黑棉衣的人和他的狗
站在茫茫的原野上了
又看远处光滑的山头了
孤零零的白杨树
没有鸟儿飞来
山也没有奔腾起来
河流也没有奔腾起来
枯黄的岸草向天边摇晃
老鹰的翅膀倾斜了
像古老的战歌一样悲壮而苍凉
起风的原野上
穿黑棉衣的人和他的狗
是北方的男子汉

Open Plain

A man in black cotton clothes with his dog

Stands on the boundless open plain

Looking at the smooth mountain peaks in the distance

The poplar trees are forlorn

No birds wing around

The mountains do not gallop

The rivers do not surge

The withered grass on the bank waves at the sky

The old eagle's wings tilt as solemn, stirring and barren as the ancient war ballad

On the windy open plain

The man in black cotton clothes with his dog

Stands a genuine man of the north

1983年

我站在北京的街道上了

1
我站在北京的街道上了
我流眼泪了

我是从小村里来的
小村很远很远
要过三条大河和很多山
也要过很多小村

我是沿着小路走来的
拐过村头的那棵皂荚树
又拐上大路
当我翻过第一道山梁的时候
就再也看不见我们的小村了

I stand on the streets of Beijing

1

I stand on the streets of Beijing
Tears gushing from my eyes

I come from a small village
A small village far, far away
I had to cross three big rivers and many mountains
and many small villages too

I came along a small path
First passing the honey locust tree at the village entrance
Turning onto the main road
When I scaled the first mountain ridge
Our little village was out of sight

但我知道
小村在那棵皂荚树下

2
我们家在小村里
小村是庄稼人的小村

小时候,祖父给我说
长大了,到大地方去
他走的最远的地方是那所小镇
他在小镇上卖过菠菜,买过猪崽
他的老婆也是在小镇上捡回来的
一个流浪的女人,从此
他又在小镇上卖祖母织的粗布了
他希望他的儿孙比他强壮
强壮地从小路走上大路
从大路走向没见过的大地方

他说北京就是最大的地方了
北京里住着皇帝
皇帝是世界上最有能耐的男人
皇帝的老婆是世界上最了不起的女人

But I knew

That little village was still beneath the honey locust tree

2

Our home is in the small village

The little village belongs to farming folk

When I was small my grandpa told me

That when I grew up I should inspect larger places

The farthest he had been was the local town

He had sold spinach and piglets there

He picked up his wife as well

She was a wandering woman, from then on

He began to sell grandma's hand-woven clothes in town

He hoped his descendents would be better off than him

Walking from small paths to big roads

Then from big roads to big places never seen before

He said Beijing was the biggest place of all

Emperors lived in Beijing

Emperors were the ablest men in the world

Their wives were the ablest women

皇帝坐的轿子

比我们村上财东杨二的还要威风

皇娘娘穿的衣服

比杨二老婆的还要气派

北京的城楼都镶着金子

北京的街道都铺着银子……

我站在北京的街道上了

我是从埋着祖父的地方来的

我想起了祖父

流眼泪了

3

北京确实很大

北京的大是祖父无法想象的

迎着那些蚂蜂一样涌来的男人和女人

我不知道,祖父会不会害怕走失

在小镇上卖菜的时候

他可是大声喊叫的啊

无拘无束地

一个男子汉的声音

The Emperor's palanquin

Was more imposing than the landlord Yang Er's in our village

The clothes the Empress wore

Were grander than Yang Er's wife's

Beijing's city towers were all clad in gold

And its streets paved with silver

I stand on the streets of Beijing

I've come from where my grandpa was buried

Recalling my grandpa

Tears streaming down

3

Beijing is really big

My grandpa couldn't imagine it

Facing those men and women surging like ants

I don't know if my grandpa would have feared them

When selling greens in the small town

He would bawl loudly

Without restraint

The authentic shout of a man

走进不再住皇帝的宫殿

我不知道,祖父会不会感到心疼

他会不会说

不住皇帝的皇宫不再是皇宫

没有皇帝的世界也不再是世界

马路为什么要那么大呢

匀一点地方不能多种点庄稼吗

花和草为什么要栽在瓦盆里呢

瓦盆不是盛盐和酱油的吗

男人和女人为什么要游游逛逛呢

游游逛逛的人会过日子吗……

我站在北京的街道上了

我是从埋着祖父的地方来的

我想起了祖父

流眼泪了

4

小村的人都知道北京

小村的人常念叨北京

小村的人都说

Walking into the palaces where the emperors no longer lived

I don't know if my grandpa would have felt heartache

Would he have said

A palace without an Emperor is not a palace any more

A world without an Emperor is not a world any more

Why are the streets so big and wide

Why not give some over to growing crops

Why plant flowers and grass in a pottery jar

Aren't jars for holding salt and soya bean sauce

Why do men and women idle around

How can idling men lead a good life …

I stand on the streets of Beijing

I've come from where my grandpa was buried

Recalling my grandpa

My eyes water

4

People in the village all know about Beijing

People in the village always natter about Beijing

People in the village all say

最有福气的人才能走到那儿

北京不知道小村
小村太小太小了
小村太远太远了
小村在那棵皂荚树下
一股风,就可以吹走小村

是小村使北京显得宽阔的啊
是小村使北京沉重的啊
是小村使北京辉煌的啊
是小村使北京成了大地方的啊

我不知道,在北京的街道上
看不见我们的小村
看不见那棵皂荚树
小村的人会不会伤心
小村的人会不会难过……

小村的人都说
最有福气的人才能走到北京
我是我们村最有福气的人了
我流眼泪了

Only the most fortunate may walk there

Beijing doesn't know about this little village

The little village is too tiny

The little village is too remote

The little village stands under the honey locust tree

A gust of wind could carry the village away

However, it is the little village that makes Beijing appear vast and wide

This little village that makes Beijing august

This little village that makes Beijing glamorous

This little village that makes Beijing a big place

On the streets of Beijing, I didn't know

There would be no sight of our little village

There would be no sight of that honey locust tree

Do the people in the small village feel heartbroken

Do the people in the small village feel sorrowful …

All the folk in the village say

Only the most fortunate can walk to Beijing

I'm the most fortunate in my village

My eyes water

5

我走了很远很远的路程
走过了三条大河和很多山
也走过了很多小村
我是从小村里来的
那里埋着我的祖父和父亲
那里住着我的妈妈

临走时,妈妈给我说
到了大地方,别忘了老家
受不了外边的生活
就回来种庄稼……

我知道
我再也不会回到小村了
我要在大地方生活了
可我是从小村里来的啊
站在北京的街道上
我流眼泪了

5

I have travelled from far, far away

Crossing three big rivers and many mountains

Any many small villages too

I came from a small village

Where my grandpa and pa are buried

Where my ma lives still

Before I left, my mother said to me

When you go to a big place, don't forget your hometown

When you cannot put up with life outside

Come home to grow crops ...

I knew

I could never go back to that small village again

I shall live in a big place

However, I came from a small village

Standing on the streets of Beijing

My eyes water

一位老人和一个孩子

一位老人和一个孩子
站在空旷的河滩上
向远处凝望

山很远
山在很远的地方
山把沉重的身影
轻轻地放在水上

山会绿,会黄
山永远不会长大
水会深,会浅
水很长很长

一位老人和一个孩子
站在空旷的河滩
风吹着老人的胡须
撩着孩子的衣裳

An Old Man and a Child

An old man and a child

Stand on the empty riverbank

Gazing into the distance

The mountain is faraway

The mountain is in a faraway place

It lies its heavy shadows

Gently on the water

The mountain may turn green and yellow

But will never grow up

The water lies deep or shallow

It runs on and on

An old man and a child

Stand on an empty riverbank

The wind caresses the old man's moustache

And parts the child's clothing

洗衣服的女人

她洗完了最后一件衣裳
她坐在石板上
小河的水清了，静了
小河水静静地流淌

她知道在她的背后
不远处，是她的村庄
她不想回去
她支着下巴儿
她要一个人坐在这儿
随便想些事情

她怎么也想不出
小河的水从哪里流来
又流到什么地方
就像不知道为什么
一个小辫子女孩儿
突然就变成了媳妇
不再叫作姑娘

The washerwoman

She finished washing the last garment
And sat down on the slate
The small river was clean and silent
Noiselessly it flowed

She knew that behind her
Not faraway, was her village
She didn't want to return
Cupping her chin with a hand
She sat there alone
Pondering random thoughts

She could not make out
Where the small river sprang from
Where it was heading
Just as she couldn't make out why
The small pigtailed girl
Suddenly turned into a wife
And was no more called a maiden

小河的水很长很长呢,她想
河水流过的地方
也一定有洗衣服的女人
她也有丈夫、孩子
从前,也是个小辫子姑娘

她真爱这个地方
她坐在石板上
她支着下巴儿
她一个人
她洗完了最后一件衣裳

She thought the waters of the small river

Ran on and on, wherever it passed

There must be washerwomen too

She had a husband, and a child as well

She too was once a small pigtailed girl

She truly adored this spot

She sat on that slate

Cupping her chin with a hand

She was alone

The last garment finished

1984年

思 念

1
离开你多少年了
仿佛又回到你的身边
你的风像温暖的手指
梳理着我的头发
黄土的气息像你
哈着我的脸……
不是你引起了我儿时的记忆
是你在淡蓝色的黄昏里
回忆我的童年

2
我的高高的城门楼呢

Longing

1

How many years have passed since I left you

It seems that I have returned to you again

Your wind like warm fingers

Combs my hair

The breath of the loess lands is like you

Breathing on my face …

It is not that you dig up my childhood memories

But you are there in the pale blue dusk

Recalling my early years

2

Where is my lofty city tower

我的霞光里摇晃的小路呢
我的书包装满快乐的故事
红高粱扬着我的布衫
我爱你那轮嫣红的落日
想起吹糖人的老汉
就听见暖暖的波浪
漫上河岸

3

田野啊,你使我多么幸福
梦里常听见你的呼唤
疲倦的时候,总想你
真想在你的怀中安眠
忘不了你每一个平静的黎明
一想起梧桐叶上的露珠
就听见温柔的钟声
向村庄问安

4

每一家门前都有一棵树
每一间屋上都有一只鸟

Where are the swaying paths in my morning glory

My satchel is stuffed with happy stories

The red sorghum flips up my clothes

I love your scarlet setting sun

I recall the old man blowing glucose figures

I hear the warm waves

Overwhelm the banks

3

Oh fields, you make me so glad

I always hear your call in my dreams

When I am tired, I always

Truly want to slumber in your bosom

The thought of the dew on the parasol tree

Brings to mind the bell's gentle peal

Giving salutations to the villages

4

There is a tree in front of every home

There is a bird atop every house

灯光温暖着纸糊的窗扇
什么事情都不会发生
一想起你迷人的夜晚
就听见父亲轻微的咳嗽
白发盖着母亲安祥的脸……

离开你多少年了呢
仿佛真回到了你的身边

The lamp warms the paper-covered windows

Nothing will happen

The thought of your charming evening

Brings to mind father's weak cough

The white hair covering mother's kind face

How many years have passed since I left you

It seems that I have returned to you again

是秋天了

赠李檬

是秋天了
淡黄色的高粱花
正奔向丰满的太阳

夏日的幻想已经过去
白杨树也带着成熟的颜色
向远处眺望
是秋天了
每一片落叶都知道了
什么叫作留恋

夜晚多么美丽
乌鸦在梧桐的阴影里
已朦胧地睡去
不知哪里飘来
泥土的气息
你就会看见月亮
还是那一枚金黄的月亮
你就会想起遥远的地方

It is Autumn now

For Li Meng

It is autumn now

The pale yellow sorghum blossom

Dashes towards the plump sun

Summer's fantasy is gone

With its mature hue, the poplar tree

Peers into the distance

It is autumn now

Every tree leaf knows

The reluctance of parting

How beautiful the night is

The crow sleeps obscurely in the shadow

Of the parasol tree

The aroma of the soil

Floats over from nowhere

Then you glimpse the moon

Still that golden moon

You will recall places faraway

想起朋友

想起家庭

老人和孩子

是秋天了

平静而不安的秋天来了

Recall your companions

Recall your kindred

Old man and child

It is autumn now

The placid yet unsettling fall has arrived

歌 手

月亮圆的时候
流浪的歌手在唱
他唱得那么忧伤
每一个村庄都在谛听
门紧紧地闭着
每一扇窗户都没有灯光

老人们说
他唱的是一件辛酸的往事
很久很久以前发生过
今后也会发生
只要河还在这里流淌
只要还有村庄
只要还有善良的人在这里死去
只要他们的儿孙还在这里生长

月亮圆的时候
流浪的歌手在唱
他唱得那么忧伤

Singer

When the moon is full
The wandering singer chants
How sorrowful his voice is
Every village listens on
With their doors tightly shut
No window has lamplight

The old man says
He sings of the plaintive past
Things which happened long ago
And maybe will occur again
As long as the river flows
As long as there are villages
As long as kind folk expire here
As long as their offspring remain

When the moon is full
The wandering singer sings
How sorrowful his voice is

梅 香

梅香抱着孩子
在屋檐下
她叫着孩子的名字
一边走一边唱歌
田野上
几个戴草帽的年轻人
望着她

他们想起了吃奶的时候
想起年轻时候的妈妈
想起有一天
也会有个黑头发女人
抱着他们的孩子
在屋檐下
美好地走来走去

这时,太阳
正照着田野上的庄稼
他们高兴得满脸通红了

Sweet Plum

Sweet Plum holds her baby

Beneath the eaves

She calls the child's name

Promenades and sings

Across in the fields

Several straw-hatted swains

Fix their eyes on her

They recall suckling their own mas

Recall their young mothers

Recall how some day in the future

There will be a black-haired woman

Holding their child

Beneath the eaves

Walking about with grace

At this moment, the sun

Beams on the crops in the field

Their faces red all over with happiness

他们扬起草帽

为她祝福

她抱着孩子，远远地

在屋檐下

They doff their straw hats

So as to bless her

She holds her child, in the distance

Beneath the eaves

朋　友

有一件事情想不开
想不开就分手了
分手得那么容易
那么痛心
一点也不后悔

确实是好朋友
有过好朋友的时光
你像爱我一样
爱过我的妻子
去过我家
那一座山
曾使你悲哀得痛哭流涕

从那以后
你再也没忘记过我
总在我意想不到的时候
出现在我的门口
站在我的面前

Friends

Taking something to heart

They went their separate ways

The parting was so easy

Yet painful

Without a shred of regret

True good friends

Savoured their time together

You loved my wife

As you loved me

You have been to my home

That mountain

Once made you sad and tearful

Henceforth

You've never forgotten me

Always appearing unexpectedly

Upon my threshold

Standing in front of me

一天天衰老
像经历了许多事情

那是些失意的日子
喝酒的时候
你把我的名字摔上桌子
喷得满是酒气

以后就是分手的日子
就是你结婚的日子
你的朋友们我不认识
也不认识那个女人
他们围在你的跟前
给你说好话
和你称兄道弟

没有我的日子
你仍旧过得那么快活
没有一点缺陷

Growing old daily

As if ripe with experience

During those frustrated days

When we were drinking

You cussed my name over the table

Spat it from a liquored-up mouth

Then came the days after we parted

And the day of your wedding

I didn't know your friends

Nor that woman

They circled around you

Spoke sweet words to you

And said you were brothers

Those days without me

You still lived with contentment

Without drawback

1985年

大青马

它是在奔跑的时候倒下的
整个高原听见了它的嘶鸣

那是一匹好马
谁知道它摔死了多少好汉
多少好汉想爬上它青色的背
享尽高原的威风
他们爱它如命怕它如命
他们摔断了所有的马鞭
一听见它的叫声
就激动得一脸铁青

那是高原上真正的马
高原人知道它的名字

The Big Black Horse

It stumbled over while galloping
The whole plateau heard it whinny

A fine steed it was, which must
Have thrown countless heroes to their deaths
Countless heroes wanted to mount it
Filled with the power and might of the prairie
Deathly was both their admiration and fear
They all flexed their whips
On hearing it whinnying
Their faces were totally blue with the thrill

That was the authentic horse of the plateau
The folk of the plateau knew its name

没有人寻找它的尸体
没有人看它死去的样子
风从山里扑来
所有的好汉都低下头去
他们知道
他们被拴在高原上了
永远走不出高原了
他们要在山口和川道
在大青马嘶鸣的地方
耗尽一生的精力

No one went to search for its body

No one caught sight of its pallor

The wind gushed out from the mountains

All the heroes bowed their heads

They knew

They were fastened to the plateau

They would never walk free from it

Where the mountain pass met the plain road

Where the big black horse whinnied

Their life-force has been spent

这些山

这些山照在画片上
就是美丽的风景
这些山拢在夜色里
就是一个和睦的家庭
这些山在高原上
是碰死好马的石头

这些山连在一起
折断你的视线
这些山挽在一起
让你迷路

那里的人吃这些山
那里的人靠这些山
他们是一群守山的人
死了,就埋在山里
埋进石头
外边的人不会知道

These mountains

When these mountains appear in pictures
They form a sumptuous scenery
When they congregate together in the evening
They form a harmonious clan
On the plateaus these mountains
Are rocks fatal to fine steeds

When these mountains chain together
They cut off your vision
When clutching each other arm-in-arm
They disorient travellers

Locals eat off these mountains
They live off these mountains
They are the custodians of the mountains
When they die they are buried in the mountains
Among the rocks
Outsiders do not know of this

没看见那些洗衣服的女人
谁知道这里会生长爱情
没看见那些晒太阳的孩子
谁知道这里还有幻想
没在山里住过
就不懂那些恨山的人
为什么在伤心的时候
想抱着山大哭一场

Without spying washerwomen

Who could know romance blooms here

Without spying sunbathing children

Who could know not fantasies breathe here

Without ever living in the mountain

People cannot understand those who hate mountains

Why they always at the heartbroken time

They want to hug the mountain and wail

石板房

每一间石板房
都能给你说点什么

晾在阳光下
躲在阴影里
给山上挂满小路
给山里点出烟火

没有这些石板房
山就让你绝望

一个石板房就是一个家庭
三个石板房就是一个寨子
一万个石板房就是一个高原

谁家的石板房亮着灯呢
谁家石板房里的女人
给她们的男人收拾行装
夜深人静的时候

House of Slate

Each house of slate

Has something to tell

Bathing beneath the sunshine

Hiding in the shadows

They tack paths onto the mountains

They exude smoke and fire in the mountains

Without these houses of slate

The mountains would cause despair

One house of slate equals one family

Three houses constitute a village

Ten thousand of them make a plateau

Which house of slate has light

The mistress of which house

Prepares a travel pack for her man

When the night is tranquil

石板房都贴着大山
变成一声不吭的石头

All the houses nudge the mountainside

And turn into a silent lump of stone

那个汉子……

那个汉子
在大车厢里勾引了你
那个汉子
在庄稼地里欺侮了你

他的胳膊蛮横有力
他的胡子蛮横有力
他的嘴巴蛮横有力
你恨死了那个汉子
你找到了那个汉子
你跟了那个汉子
一辈子,然后是一辈子
你再也没想过什么

That Macho Man

That macho man

He seduced you on the big cart

That macho man

He bullied you among the crops

His arms were rude and powerful

His moustache was rude and powerful

His mouth was rude and powerful

You hate him to death

You found him

You followed him

All your life, and then all your life

You never thought of anything else

老　家

1
一方水土养一方人
住惯了
就守在那儿
不再离开
那儿就成了家
就有了好风水

2
是一条水
还是一架山
是一座庙宇
还是一棵树
也许是瓷器
也许是水果
每个地方都有一样好东西
让那里的人

Hometown

1

One place nurtures one person

Growing accustomed to it

You stay there

Never leaving

That place becomes home

And enjoys great geomantic omen

2

Is it a river

Or a mountain

Is it a temple

Or a tree

Perhaps it is pottery

Perhaps it is fruit

Each place has its local delicacy

Let the faces of the folk

一辈子脸上生辉

3
老家有姑婆陵
姑婆是个有名的女人
她当过皇帝
她躺在姑婆陵里
躺得很有福气
一条河从她的脚下流过去
河水流过的地方
是一片平原

4
老家有个好名字
老家叫乾州
乾就是天
老家人靠天吃饭
老家人以庄稼为生
他们交公粮纳税
干旱的日子
他们就说

Be radiant for a lifetime

3

Great aunt's tomb is in my hometown

Great aunt was an eminent lady

She was a female emperor

She lay in her mausoleum

With satisfaction

A river flows past beneath her feet

The place where the river runs

Is a vast plain

4

My hometown had a name

It was called the Qian prefecture

Qian means "the heavens"

Locals lived off the heavens

Locals survived on the crops

They paid taxes and grain to the state

When they ran into drought

They would say

老天不给人吃饭了哎
他们就看看天

5
他们以善心待人
他们委曲求全
他们也结交朋友
好朋友就是他们的邻家
他们就像树根一样
纠缠在一起
一个人死了
就惊动全村
他们说
十个亲戚不如一个好邻家
他们说
兔子不吃窝边草

6
出远门的人
回到老家
他们像亲人一样

"The heavens are refusing us a meal"

And raise their eyes skyward

5

They treated others with kindness

Making compromises for the common good

They made friends

Good friends were their neighbours

Like tree roots

They intertwined with each other

When a person died

The whole village shared the shock

They would say

"Ten relatives are no better than one good neighbour"

They would say

"Rabbits do not eat grass around their own warren"

6

When one who has travelled afar

Returns to his hometown

People treat him

他们打招呼
他们说动心的话
他们真好
他们的心是肉长的
他们可怜出门的人
他们认定在外边一定受苦
他们都说
好出门不如歹在家

7
他们羡慕当官的人
他们害怕当官的人
他们离不开当官的人
没人管他们的时候
他们就不会过日子了
不知道路该怎么走了
他们是一群可怜的虫虫
夏天，他们把衣服脱在地坎上
冬天，他们把手缩在袖子里

8
他们有许多忌讳

As their own kin

Their words are heartfelt

They are genuinely fine

Their heart emanates through their flesh

They show pity to him who has travelled afar

They are certain his sufferings were great outside

They would all say

"A good life outside is no better than a wretched home-life"

7

They admired those officials

They feared those officials

They could not live without officials

When nobody took charge of them

They knew not how to live a life

How to walk along the road

They were pitiful worms

In summer, they threw their clothes on the ground

In winter, they tucked their hands into their sleeves

8

They had so many taboos

要上县城卖菜了

要去北山换粮了

他们就赶个早起

他们怕碰上女人

他们说出门的时候

碰上女人一定晦气

9
大地方的人会笑他们

说他们是些冒傻气的人

就凭着那股子傻气

他们一辈子安分守己

他们说人要知足

他们说好死不如赖活着

10
明天呢

他们说谁知道明天

是个什么样子

往前的路是黑的

上山么——打柴

They would go to the county town to sell greens

They would go to the northern mountains to swap grains

They would start early

They feared running into women

They said when going out

"Bad luck ensues from encountering a dame"

9

People from big places would laugh at them

And say they were silly

Their silliness would cause them

To be always content with their lot

They said man must be content with his lot

Even a good death is no match for a wretched existence

10

What about tomorrow

They say who knows

What tomorrow will be

The road ahead is dark

Climbing the mountain — to collect firewood

过河么——脱鞋
他们总这么说这么说

11
他们也有幻想
他们把希望
放在儿孙身上
也许有那么一天
到了儿孙手里
就会出人头地
三十年河东
三十年河西
他们总这么说这么说

12
老家就是这么个地方
老家人就这样
守在那里
守着姑婆陵
守着他们的过活
哪怕发生天大的事情

Crossing the river — you first take off your shoes

They constantly spoke in this way

11

They also had their fantasies

They pinned their hopes

On their offspring

Perhaps some day in the future

Their offspring

Would rise head and shoulders above the rest

Thirty years on the east riverbank

Thirty years on the west

They constantly spoke in this way

12

My hometown was such a place

The folk were just like this

They kept on guard

Kept on guarding great aunt's mausoleum

Kept on guarding their lives there

Even if the heavens and earth swapped places

也能把穷难日子
过得温暖

They would make their hardscrabble life

Become warm and cozy

大西北

玛纳斯湖在刮风
博斯腾湖在刮风
青海湖在刮风
鄂陵湖扎陵湖在刮风
准噶尔在刮风
塔里木柴达木在刮风
天山昆仑山祁连山在刮风
古尔班通古特在刮风
塔克拉玛干在刮风
巴丹吉林和腾格里在刮风
河西走廊在刮风
乌鲁木齐兰州银川西宁在刮风
黄土高原在刮风
起风了
黄帝陵秦皇陵昭陵乾陵在刮风
霍去病的石马在刮风
胡笳羌笛古筝编钟在刮风
飞天的长袖在刮风
生在这儿长在这儿活在这儿要刮风

The Great Northwest

Wind blows over Manas Lake

Wind blows over Basten Lake

Wind blows over Qinghai Lake

Winds blows over Eling and Zhaling Lakes

Wind blows over the Junggar Basin

Wind blows over Tarim and qaidam Basin

Wind blows over Mounts Tian, Kunlun, and Qilian

Wind blows over the Gurbantunggut Desert

Wind blows over the Taklimakan Desert

Wind blows over Badanjaran and Tengger

Wind blows through the Hexi Corridor

Wind blows through Urumqi, Lanzhou, Yinchuan, and Xining

Wind blows over the Loess Plateau

The wind rises

It blows over the tombs of the Yellow Emperor

The First Qin Emperor, Taizong and Lady Wu

It blows over Huo Qubing's stone horse statuary

It blows through the Hujia pipes, the Qiang's flute

The Chinese ancient zither and chimes

死在这儿埋在这儿塑在这儿要刮风
几千年前一万年后要刮风
大西北是刮风的地方
大西北就是一股风

西北人在刮风的地方喝酒
西北人在刮风的地方造屋
西北人吃大块牛肉羊肉马肉
西北人点一堆火就烧熟骆驼
西北人生男儿生女儿
长大了就是西北人不会断子绝孙
西北人死了就埋进沙漠埋进戈壁
埋进随便哪一块地方不说什么
西北人敢和汉武帝唐太宗打仗
打赢了就烧就夺就抢
就让蔡文姬做他们头人的老婆
西北人失败了也是英雄
就让人家杀让人家割让人家宰
就让战马长啸让大雪扑满弓刀
西北人让儿孙们走进北京走进上海
走进杭州苏州扬州当丈夫当主妇
让全中国生长他们的骨血
西北人不敢碰见西北人

It blows against the flying sleeves of the Dunhuang dancer
The wind blows here when you are born, grow up and live
The wind blows here when you die, are buried, and memorialized with statues
The wind blew here thousands of years ago and ten thousand years hence
The Great Northwest is a place with wind
The Great Northwest is gust of wind

Northwesterners drink liquor in this windy place
Northwesterners build houses in this windy place
Northwesterners eat hefty joints of mutton, beef, and horse
Northwesterners can roast camels on a pyre
Northwesterners give birth to boys and girls
They grow up to be northwesterners, carrying on the bloodline
Northwesterners die and are buried in the Gobi Desert
Any place can form their burial ground
Northwesterners dared to fight Emperor Wu of Han and Taizong of Tang
When victorious they would sack and loot and rob
And made Wenji Cai the wife of their chief
Even when defeated they were heroes still
They let themselves be bullied and killed freely by others
They let their steeds roar and arrows and knives be covered in snow

一碰见就会碰出一团火

碰出天山祁连山昆仑山

碰出毡房碰出拴马桩

碰出酒泉

碰出那一块刮风的地方

碰出一条倒淌河

西北人一个女人一顶帐篷

一群马一群孩子就是一个家

西北人一脸土一脸灰但不晦气

西北人穷得丁当硬得丁当

走到天尽头也能认得出

西北人打老婆骂老婆

出远门就想老婆

野男人拐走老婆就想动刀子

就闷在屋里喝酒

喝完酒就原谅了老婆

西北人开羊肉馆开牛肉馆

招揽天下人

西北人爱唱花儿爱唱道情爱弹冬不拉

西北人爱听板胡爱唱秦腔红脖子涨脸

西北人走几天见不着村庄见不着人影

就一个人自言自语

Northwesterners allowed their offspring to walk to Beijing and Shanghai

To be husbands and wives in Hangzhou, Suzhou and Yangzhou

Let their blood spread all over China

Northwesterners dare not encounter their folk

When they meet they clank out fire

Clank out Mounts Tian, Qilian and Kunlun

Clank out yurts and hitching posts

Clank out the liquor fountain

Clank out a windswept place

Clank out the backflow of a river

One northwestern woman makes a tent

A group of horses and infants form a family

Northwesterners' faces may be filled with earth and ash but never misfortune

Northwesterners are penniless yet brave

One could pick them out even if you walked to the ends of the earth

They curse and beat their wives

But miss them when they travel afar

When cuckolded they reach for their knives

And sup gloomily in their chamber

Mustering forgiveness when that bout is over

西北人在大沙漠大戈壁

在大山里异想天开

西北人要住楼房要乘电梯

要在漂亮的街道上遛达

西北汉子要娶漂亮姑娘

生漂亮儿子过漂亮日子

西北人想打电话想坐飞机

想知道天下事

西北人想爬上火车出潼关经河南

一夜间开进青岛开进太平洋

西北人吃一辈子苦一辈子一辈子

一辈子没怨过这个世界……

起风了
大西北在刮风

Northwesterners operate mutton and beef restaurants

Entertain everyone under the sun

They love Gansu arias, Shanxi opera and playing the tambouras

Listening to the banhu and singing Shaanxi opera red-faced

They perhaps will walk several days spying neither villages nor folk

So resort to talking to themselves

Northwesterners inhabit the Great Desert and the Gobi

Fantasize within the deep mountains

They want to live in high buildings with elevators

To stroll along beautiful streets

Their men want to marry beautiful maidens

Have beautiful babies and lead beautiful lives

Northwesterners want to use phones and fly in planes

To know about everything under the sun

To board the train as far as Tong Pass, then tour Henan

Reach Qingdao and the Pacific in a single night

Northwesterners bear hardships their whole lives long

But never complain about this world at any stage …

The wind rises

The wind blows over the Great Northwest

1986年

黄土高原（六首）

> 黄土高原位于中国西北部，跨青海、甘肃、宁夏、陕西、山西、河南六省市，面积五十三万平方公里，为世界最大黄土高原。古生代时期，这里是一片汪洋；古生代末期，它开始破水而出，呈现优美的亚热带风光。第四纪，强大的西北风把蒙古高原以至中亚地区的尘状粉沙向东南搬迁，历数十万年的日积月累，这里被覆盖上了一层黄土。这里也有太阳、月亮、河流。也有许多人住在这里……
>
> ——题记

大风弥漫

你从大睡中醒来
腰仰起又弯下
像一根柔韧的弓
你甩动长发

The Loess Plateau (Six Pieces)

The Loess Plateau is located in the northwestern region of China. It stretches across six provinces — Qinghai, Gansu, Ningxia, Shaanxi, Shanxi and Henan – and covers an area of 530, 000 square kilometres. It is the largest loess plateau in the world. During the Palaeozoic Era it was filled with a boundless ocean. During the later Palaeozoic Era it started to rise out of the water and be transformed into a magnificent subtropical landscape. In the Quaternary Period the strong northwestern wind began to transport dust and sand particles from Mongolia and Central Asia so that after millions of years of accumulation the region became covered with loess. It is home to the sun, the moon and rivers, and people live here also…

The wind gusts all over

You wake from sleeping soundly

向我呵气

遥远的西北方

响着你空阔的呼吸

你揉捏母岩

揉捏干旱的草原和戈壁

指缝间金灿灿的畜粉飘飘扬扬

吹向我

吹向我

吹我的褶皱

吹我的臂弯

吹我最羞涩的地方

起风了起风了

大风弥漫

风尘纷纷降落

让我不安地扭动

让我丰满

让我荒凉

让我赤身裸体地躺在这儿

作塬的样子

作梁的样子

作峁的样子

引诱太阳

引诱痛苦的眼睛

Your back straightens and curves

Like a supple bow

You shake your long hair

Puff at me

Your vast breath

Echoes through the huge northwest

You crush the mother rock into pieces

Crush the dry prairie and Gobi into pieces

Golden powder dances between your fingers

Blows towards me

Towards me

Blows over my wrinkles

Over my arms

And over my shyest places

The wind rises, the wind rises

The wind gusts all over

The dust descends

Making me wriggle with unease

Making me plump

Making me desolate

Making me lie there stark naked

In the form of a plateau

风啊

大风弥漫……

太　阳

你把淫威温和地泼给我

像我的男人

给我灿烂的鼻息

给我灿烂的手掌

给我灿烂的芒刺

照亮我每一个地方

让我呻吟

让我裂开

让我干巴巴

让我渴

你嗅我的身体

你在我的身上写字

你在我的身上画画

我不说一句话

干巴巴的眼窝张着

干巴巴的嘴唇张着

In the form of a ridge

In the form of a hilltop

Seducing the sun

Seducing sad eyes

Oh, the wind

The wind gusts all over...

The Sun

You sprinkle your despotic power over me

Like my man

Offering me brilliant nasal breath

Offering me brilliant palms

Offering me brilliant thorns

Light up every part of me

Make me groan

Make me crack

Make me dry

You smell my body

You scribble on my body

You paint on my body

我渴

太阳
太阳滚圆

泥　河

海退潮时留下你

留下浑浊的胸音

在我的低处呜咽

震动我

冲击我

切割我

汛期如约来临

你和季节合谋

用优美的线条

奔跑着给我纹身

让我绝望

让我沉沦

让我闭上眼睛

习惯你

像习惯日落日升

习惯过去的每一个日子一样

I do not say a word

My dry eyes are wide open

My dry mouth is agape

I am thirsty

The sun

The round ball of the sun

River mud

You left when the tide receded

Left your turbid chest sounds

Sobbing in my low place

Make me vibrate

Lash out at me

Flay me open

The flood came as expected

You conspired with the season

Using eloquent lines

Dashing to tattoo me

To make me disappear

To make me sink

To make me close my eyes

习惯你堂皇的勒索

我的黄土漫无边际

随你凹陷

随你脱落

像树叶随风

随你走

随你流

随你蜿蜒

明月降临

记不清什么时候

什么时候你已降临

波浪在我的指尖上悄然开放

开放又流淌

一群群白蝴蝶如醉如迷

只有你降临的时候

我才是柔软的女人

我的树才朦朦胧胧

让风拨动

我的草叶才宽舒地伸开

鸟儿睡在梦的边缘

我的小路摇摇晃晃

And grow as accustomed to you

As I am to sunrise and sunset

As I am to each passing day

As I am to your magnificent extortion

My loess is endless

It lets you undulate at will

It lets you shake yourself off at will

Like leaves following the wind

Walking with you

Floating with you

Zigzagging with you

The Bright Moon Ascends

I cannot remember clearly

When you made your descent

The waves silently blossom on my fingertips

Blossom and flow by

Groups of intoxicating white butterflies

Only when you were ascending

I am a soft woman

My trees would be obscurely

Wind-shaken

爬上山又爬下山

河流轻如呼吸

在我的手背上

灾难只是影子

遥远又遥远

记不清什么时候

什么时候你已降临

让我迷蒙

让我寥廓

让我苍茫如水如烟

树　王

你精心地收集月光

收集又滑落

泼上我的胸膛犹如泼墨

你用苍绿的叶子

给我作海的颜色

作波浪的轻响

让我听鱼类的声音

让我听贝壳的声音

让我听鹦鹉螺的声音

My leaves would spread contentedly

The birds slumbered on the edge of a dream

My path swayed here and there

Climbing up and down the mountains

The river was as light as breath

On the back of my hand

Disasters are only shadows

Further and further away

I cannot remember clearly

When you made your descent

Making me perplexed

Making me lonely

Making me boundless as water and smoke

King of the Trees

You collected moonlight elaborately

Collected and let it slide away again

Sprinkled it on my chest like ink

You used dark green leaves

To make the colour of the sea

Make the soft sound of the waves

海百合抖动裙裾

在幽蓝处开放

珊瑚的珠光闪闪烁烁

你摇起青葱的帆缆

让我想起雨季来临时

蕨类快活的模样

蒿类快活的模样

莎草科和栎属类快活的模样

金黄的大雨滂沱

金黄的阳光滂沱

滂沱如金黄的瀑布

羚羊和三趾马越过世纪的栅栏

响过浅水湖

辽阔的草原让我酥软

你用手指刺痛我

风舔噬着我的额头

生命被一茬茬收割

挤压在我的墙壁

剥落如叶如鳞

飞起的不是鹰

是风化的石燕

你在荒凉的庭院里

向一贫如洗的天空震响

Let me listen to the sound of the fish

Let me listen to the sound of the shell

Let me listen to the sound of the nautilus

The sea lily shook the edge of its skirt

Blossomed in a dark blue region

The coral shone with its pearly light

You swung your green onion like sail rope

Making me recall how when the rainy season came

How lively the ferns were

How lively the wormwood was

How lively the flatsedge and oak were

The golden downpour comes in torrents

The golden sunshine comes in torrents

Like a golden waterfall

The takin and hipparion cross the fences of the century

Echoes over the shallow lake

The vast grassland makes me limp and soft

Your fingers stab me painfully

The wind licks my forehead

Life was harvested one crop after another

Squeeze into my walls

Shake off like leaves and scales

What flies up is not an eagle

让我回头

让我沉默

风干的黄泥无边无沿

高原人

黑压压一片面目肮脏的是你们么

太阳晒黄风吹着的是你们么

交公粮纳税唱酸曲的是你们么

和山和黄土结下冤仇的是你们么

是你们卑琐的一群

把头垂在胸前

垂在两手之间

守着我死也不肯离开

来吧你们

爬上我的胸膛

给你肥嫩的草

给你高粱

给你糜谷

给你过不完的日子

我养你

喂你

But a fossilized swallow

In your desolate courtyard

It echoes in the poor heaven

Make me turn my head back

Make me silent

The dried yellow mud is endless and edgeless

People of the Plateau

Aren't you the dark group with dirty faces

Aren't you the group blown by the yellow wind and tanned by the sun

Aren't you the group paying state taxes with grain and singing bawdy ballads

Aren't you the group who feuds with mountains and yellow earth

You are a petty and low group

Your heads dangle before your chests

Between your hands

You would rather die than leave me unguarded

Come all of you

Climb onto my chest

I'll offer you lush tender grass

Offer you sorghum

埋你
什么也不留下

就这么你们
把头垂在你们的胸前
垂在两手之间
以生命家族中最痛苦的姿势
朝向我
占有我
占有我金黄的躯体
让时间缓缓流过

Offer you millet

Offer you endless days of life

I shall raise you

Feed you

And bury you

Leaving no trace behind

In this fashion

You dangle your head in front of your chest

Between your hands

In the most sorrowful position of your clan

Face me

Occupy me

Occupy my golden body

Let time elapse slowly

牡丹台

1
全世界的月光
好像都集中在这里了
照着牡丹台
守护着她

站在牡丹台的高处
能看见罗子山
能听见黄河的声音
黄河像冻僵的指头
裂开一道口子
一路而下
那里有筏子和摆渡的船夫
牡丹台的人不认识他们

2
牡丹台在沟掌里

Peony Pavilion

1

All the moonlight in the world

The moonlight of the whole world

Seems focused on here

Shining on the peony pavilion

And guarding her

Standing on the top of the peony pavilion

I can see the Luozi Hill

Hear the sound of the Yellow River

Like frozen fingers

Cracked and chapped

It gushes along its course

With rafts and ferrymen

Unbeknownst to those in the peony pavilion

2

The peony pavilion stands in the palm of the valley

离它最近的村子

要走二十里

二十里路上都是石头

两边也是石头

石头抵着天

石头上长满松树

让人害怕

也让人迷离

走这样的路

会以为它能通往仙地

到牡丹台就会看见

那里没有神仙

有人在坡上犁地

有人在沟底种蒜

3

很早以前

一户河南人来到这里

不想走了

就放下挑子

在这里安了家

The nearest village

Is twenty itdics away

That twenty itdics of road is covered with stones

Stones line both sides as well

Touching as far as the sky

Accommodating pine trees

Inspiring fear

And perplexity

Walking on such a road

People may think they are going to a fairyland

When they reach the peony pavilion they can see

No fairies are there No fairy is there

People plough the slope

People grow garlic on the valley floor

3

Long ago

A family from Henan came here

And didn't want to leave

They laid down their carrying pole

And set up home, hence

牡丹台就有了人声
有了淡蓝的炊烟

以后又来了一户
又来了一户
就这么
牡丹台有了七户人家
七户人说着三个省的话

那时候
牡丹台上开满了野牡丹
现在没有了
牡丹开花的地方
开了荒
种了庄稼

4
牡丹台没有学校
孩子们都会捏尿泥
也会过家家
长大了就满沟里跑
看见外边进来的人

The peony pavilion resounds with human life

And teal kitchen smoke billows

Later, along came another family

And then one more

Thus

Seven families came to reside in the peony pavilion

Seven families speaking the dialects of three provinces

At that time

The pavilion was decked in wild peonies

But now none remain

In the place where peonies bloomed

The wasteland has been opened up

For growing crops

4

There is no school at the peony pavilion

Children mix their pee and mud into playdough

Make-believe at being husbands and wives

When they grow-up they race across the valley floor

Spotting outsiders

他们就瞪着黑眼睛

看见一只狼

也没有这么惊奇

没人愿意嫁到这里

可这里的人也有爱情

你娶我家的女子

我嫁你家的汉子

七户人就这么

做了亲戚

有了血肉联系

5

不知什么时候

牡丹台也有了一个队长

七户人都听他的

他是牡丹台的老户

娶了七户里最漂亮的姑娘

只有牡丹台的人知道

他有多么重要

牡丹台是一只船

They stare at them with dark eyes

Being not quite so surprised

When a wolf puts in an appearance

Nobody wants to marry the folk from here

But people here have love of their own

You marry off your daughter to us

And you gain our son

So the seven families

All became kinsman

And wrought ties of blood

5

Nobody remembers now, but

The peony pavilion production brigade once had a leader

Who was listened to by all seven families

Coming from the earliest settlers

He married the bonniest girl among the seven clans

Only the people of the pavilion knew

How important he was

Were the peony pavilion an ark

他就是掌舵的

牡丹台是一个国家

他就是皇帝

他让牡丹台的人

有了尊卑贵贱

也有了等级

6

白天在远处看

牡丹台悄儿没声

晚上在近处听

牡丹台悄儿没声

收获的季节

就有人来到这里

让他们把公粮拉到那个小镇

走五十里山路

交给粮店

这时候

你就会知道

牡丹台不是世外桃园

He would be the pilot

Were the peony pavilion a country

He would be the emperor

He made the people there

Know what humility and nobility were

And comprehend class difference

6

In the daytime, looking from afar

The peony pavilion was tranquil

In the evening to a listener from nearby

The peony pavilion was tranquil

During the harvest season

Someone would come here

Asking them to carry grains as tax to the town

Travel fifty itdics along the mountain road

To offer it to the state granary

At this time

You will know

The peony pavilion was no peach blossom paradise

牡丹台在中国

是中国的一个村子

想想这个

真让人惊叹

7

也说不定有一天

这里会出一个名人

牡丹台就和每一个

出名人的地方一样了

会写进书里

被许多人提起

让许多人向往

牡丹台的石头就成了好石头

牡丹台的黑窑洞

就成了世界上最好的窑洞

It was in China

A village in China

Thinking of this

Really startled people

7

Maybe some day hence

An eminent person will emerge from here

As they do from any other place

The peony pavilion will be described in books

Mentioned by many readers

Longed for by many outsiders

Then the stones of the pavilion will become precious

The dark caverns there

Will become the finest cave-rooms in the world

鼓　阵

白羊肚手巾涨潮了
窑里生的沟里长的风里吹的
庄稼汉涨潮了

酸倒牙酸倒石头专惹婆姨汉子
站着听坐着听眼睛瞪着心里痒着的酸曲
偏偏不唱要敲这牛皮腰鼓
风里响雨里响糜谷一样金黄透亮
嫁女子迎媳妇过川道进拐沟
在向阳的坡上出殡送葬的唢呐
偏偏不吹要敲这牛皮腰鼓
不飘飘洒洒不袅袅娜娜
就这么闷声闷气地踏踏踏踏
震这些走不出看不透的黄土峁峁沟沟岔岔
不颤颤悠悠不飞飞扬扬
就这么一槌一声地咚叭咚叭
震你手震你胳膊
震得你心里忽儿忽儿地

Drum Formation

The ovine white tower rose up like a tide

The cave-born farmers grew up in the valley

Weathered by the wind, rising up like a tide

They won't sing bawdy ballads

Which stir the hearts of men and women

Embarrassing even teeth and stones

It is the custom to listen to them

Sitting and standing, one's eyes wide open

And heart itching

Refusing to sing

They beat a cowhide drum

They won't blow the suona pipe

Which echoes in the wind and rain as gold as millet

Echoes among the wedding parties

Zigzagging through gulleys and plain paths

Echoes among the funeral processions

On the sunny slope

They refuse to blow

Preferring the cowhide drum

Without natural grace and elegance

Just pit-patting in a muffled way

Arresting the gulleys and valleys

Never leaving this place

Without shivering and floating

Just pit-patting one at a time

Arresting your hands and arms

Arresting your heart and stirring it

In this way it passed in and out of the valleys and ditches

The ovine white tower rose up like a tide

In this way it went up and down the slopes and ridges

The farmers rose up like a tide

In this way they jumped high and knocked,

Their eyes red and their blood warm

In this way they jumped and jumped

With their hearts puzzled, then painful and puzzled again

Puzzling like this and feeling pain like this

What the pain and puzzle are about is a mystery

The little grindstone by the cave door

Could not tell

就这么来了来了进了壕壕出了壕壕

白羊肚手巾涨潮了

就这么来了来了上了坡坡下了坡坡

庄稼汉涨潮了

就这么敲着敲着眼红了血热了跳得老高老高

就这么跳着跳着心迷了心疼了心疼了又心迷了

就这么迷了又疼疼了又迷什么也说不清了

窑门口的小石磨说不清了

甩蹄子的小毛驴说不清了

墙上挂的窑里摆的牛鞭羊鞭老镢头

破皮袄酸菜缸子和大头苍蝇说不清了

栽多少杨树柳树槐树还是光秃秃

落不住一根鸟毛的峁峁梁梁坡坡说不清了

崖畔上窑畔上姑娘后生一堆一堆说不清了

路上想好事炕上说好事睡觉梦好事

一辈子遇几回好事说不清了

踏踏踏踏涨潮了

咚叭咚叭涨潮了

哭说不清了

笑说不清了

一肚子红萝卜土豆红薯

和一肚子的晦气闷气运气说不清了

坡上埋的炕上供的就是爷爷奶奶祖先们

The small donkey kicking its hooves

Could not tell

The cow whip, sheep whip and hoe

Hanging on the cave wall

Could not tell

The worn fur coats

The big pickle jar and the large-headed flies

Could not tell

The gulleys and valleys, which would remain always barren

No matter how many willows and poplars grew

These could not capture a single bird's feather

Could not tell

The young man and girl in groups

On the clifftop and the cave top

Could not tell

Those who imagine heartening thoughts on the road

Those who chatter about good things on the itdics

Those who dream about positive tidings in their sleep

Could not tell how much good fortune

They would run into through their whole lives

Itdics, itdics, the tide rises

Itdics, itdics, the tide rises

You cannot tell how much weeping

臭鞋烂袜子盆盆罐罐和酸甜苦辣说不清了

怀里抱的手里拖的就是后辈儿孙一代又一代

流多少鼻涕眼泪

长大了就守在这里娶婆姨嫁汉子

种糜子谷子吃谷子糜子

也许想出人头地就说不清了

祖坟埋到好处的就走出去

到北京到上海到西安到那些大地方

当大官当大人物指手画脚不再回来

一提起就让一沟的人脸上发光也说不清了

就这么一声不吭地踏踏踏踏

涌过来了涌过来了

白羊肚手巾涨潮了

就这么不言不语地咚叭咚叭

涌过来了涌过来了

庄稼汉涨潮了

就这么让你不知道想哭还是想笑血就热了

就这么让你见上一回

心里就忽儿忽儿地

一辈子也忘不了了……

You cannot tell how much laughter

You cannot tell how many carrots

Potatoes and sweet potatoes

And how much poor luck

There is in your stomach

Those you buried on the slope

And worshipped on the itdics

Are you grandparents and ancestors

You cannot tell how many reeking shoes, torn socks

And jars full of sweet, sour, bitter, and spicy flavours

You possess in your arms and hands

Are generation after generation of offspring

You cannot tell how much nasal mucus

They will shed

When they grow up

They will marry men and women

Here and guard this place

Growing and eating millet

You cannot tell

If they want to stand above others

Those who bury their ancestors

安平

With favourable itdics go out

To big cities like Beijing, Shanghai, and Xi'an

To become major officials and big-shots

And never return

The very mention of them

Makes the valley folks' faces shine

In this way, they just chit chat

With muffled voices

Roaming over, roaming over

The ovine white tower rose like the tide

In this way they thumped, thumped

Without breathing a word

Roaming over, roaming over

The farmers rose like tides

In this way they make your blood warm

And make you unable to tell

Whether you want to cry or laugh

In this way when seeing them

Only once

Your heart will stir

Being unable to forget them

As long as you live …

窗 花

窗上总糊着麻纸
她说
山里风大

年好过
月好过
她说
日子难过

一年吃一回肉
吃肉的时候
麻纸就贴上窗花

狮子滚绣球啦
喜鹊闹梅花啦
蓝鱼儿张着嘴巴
还有一只猫
她说
猫儿会叫春呢

Papercut on the window

The window was always covered with brown paper

She said

The mountain wind is strong

One year is easily spent

One month is easily spent

She said

But each day is a grind

Once a year they eat meat

When they do so

They decorate the window with papercuts

Lions playing with a ball

Magpies chirping on plum boughs

Blue fish opening their mouths wide

There was also a cat

She said

The cat was able to mew on heat

跟娘学会了这个
那时候
还是个女子家

好看么
她跪在炕头上
穿件破褂儿
一笑才看见
不知道什么时候
掉了几颗牙

It learned that from my mother

Is it beautiful

She knelt on the edge of the itdics

Wearing a worn overcoat

When she smiled

She realised, though she hadn't known

Several of her teeth were gone

那个人

她一个人
在坡地里看天
布衫上流着风

没有云彩
还是那个太阳
鹰儿抖翅膀呢
她想

帽子放在磨顶上……
鞭子挂在钉钉上……

是拦牛的老汉
唱酸曲呢
唱得人心慌

她一个人
卷着裤腿
在坡地里看天

That man

She was alone

Looking at the sky from the tilting field

Wind billowing her blouse

There were no clouds

The sun remained unchanged

The eagle shook its wings

She thought

The hat was on the top of the grindstone …

The whip was hanging on the nail …

The old cowherd

Was singing a bawdy ballad

Which made hearts stir

She was alone

With her trousers rolled up

Looking at the sky from the tilting field

金灿灿的黄土

富贵又荒凉

就她一个人

在坡地里看天

The golden yellow earth

Was both rich and desolate

She was alone

Looking at the sky from the tilting field

雪花的孩子

雪花的孩子
在硷畔上
不哭也不闹
她是雪花的孩子
雪花正在碾米
一边赶毛驴儿
一边看着她

总有那么一天
她到底会长大
到底会知道那些山
那些石头
可现在
她只是雪花的孩子
是个小姑娘
在硷畔上
不哭也不闹

Snowflake's Child

Snowflake's child

Was on the clifftop

Neither weeping nor pestering

She was Snowflake's child

Snowflake was grinding millet

While driving the donkey

She looked at her

Someday in the future

She will grow up at last

She would know about the mountains

And the stones

But at the moment

She was only Snowflake's child

A little girl

On the clifftop

Who neither wept nor pestered

憩 息

他们坐着
在梢林里憩息
棉袄使他们变得臃肿
阳光穿过空隙
涂抹着他的脸
他张着眼睛
听见她
解开辫子的声音

年轻的时候
他爬过许多山
才知道还有许多山
用尽一生的力气
也爬不出去
山不给人一点希望
他真想跳进去
让山淹死

就这么

A Short Break

They are sitting there

At the edge of the forest, having a short break

Swelled by their cotton-padded clothes

The sunshine darts through the empty space

Painting their faces

He opens wide his eyes

He hears the sound

Of her untying her pigtail

When young

He climbed so many mountains

Then realised they were too numerous

Even if he expended his whole life force

He could never climb free

The mountains offered no hope

He really wanted to bound among them

And be drowned by them

In this way

他折过身

敲开她家的窑门

显出很累的样子

现在他们坐着

在梢林里

是一对砍柴的夫妻

梢林空空洞洞的

像经历了许多时光

他张着眼睛

听见她

解开辫子的声音

He turned around

And knocked her door open

Appearing exhausted

Now the pair are sitting

At the edge of the forest

They are a couple cutting firewood

It is empty at the edge of the forest

As if so much time has passed

He opens wide his eyes

And hears the sound

Of her untying her pigtail

1987年

屋檐水

1
就这么
坐在我跟前
围绕我
淹没我,无声无息
看着我
想流泪的样子
就这么
让我感到
我是个孩子

2
我怕,怕我的愚笨

Water from the Eaves

1

Sit beside me

Around me

Drown me, silently

Look at me

In the attitude of shedding tears

In this way

Let me feel

I am a child

2

I fear, fear that I am foolish

Cannot offer you glee

不能给你欢愉

怕树叶在窗口

意外地凋谢

你会想起另一个时间

另一个地点

有一样东西正在跌落

你就离开我

怕你离开的时候

不留下什么

3

只有这间小屋

一杯清水

一堆烟蒂

只有你的声音

温顺地流着,让我

不再感动

不再难过

也不再说话

我仅仅是在享受

Fear that the leaves at the window

Will wither unexpectedly

You might believe that at another time

In another place

Something was falling off

3

Only this small room

A cup of clean water

A heap of cigarette butts

Only the sound of you

Gently dripping leaves me

No longer touched

No longer sad

No longer talkative

I am simply savouring this

4

You are always willing

Let me kiss you

But don't let me look

4
你总是情愿地
让我吻你
不让我看见

你有些努力
你总是忽略
一些话题
让我感激
让我痛苦地感到
没有遥远的地方

5
你只是看着我
看我写字
看我抽烟
看我抽烟的时候
消瘦的姿势
让我忘记
我们正在相爱
我们只是

You try hard

You always neglect

Certain topics

Make me grateful

Let me rue how

There is no distant place

5

You just look at me

Look at me writing

Look at me smoking

Look at my gaunt posture

When I am smoking

Make me forget

We are in love

We are only

Sharing an experience

You always lightly

Perfectly share my mind

在经历着什么

你总是这么平淡地
和我默契

6
你总是在我需要的时候
把手伸给我
把头靠在我的胸前
胆怯地看我
脸上的泪水
一点也不做作

你总是默默地参与我的疼痛
让我无话可说

7
这是我美好的时辰
没有什么会打扰我
雨水悄无声息
落在每一条路上

6

You always stretch out your hand to me

When I am in need

Lean your head against my chest

Peeping shyly at me

The tears on your face

Are never affected

You always share

My pain in silence

Having nothing to say to me

7

This is my optimum time

Nothing interrupts me

Silently the rainwater

Drops onto every road

On each road

There are people walking home

This is the time to walk home

This is the time I am alone

每一条路上

都有人走回家去

这是回家的时候

这是我一个人的时候

这是我孤独的时候

只有这时候

我才能细致一些

潜心一些，点一支烟

在我的小屋里

不激动

也不等待

这是我想你的时候

8
就这么

贴着我的脸

不说话

给我的只是气息

想起我

有多么的想你

就这么

This is the time I am lonely

Only at this moment

Can I grow more delicate

Perfect concentration, light a cigarette

In my small room

I am not excited

I am not expectant

This is the time when I miss you

8

Touch my face

In this way

Speak not a word

Only give me your breath

To recall

How much I miss you

In this way I am made

Unable to tear myself away

Let me recall, let me

Think over everything

When I have lost you

让我依恋
让我回忆，让我
在失去你的时候
什么都会想起

别让我失去
别让我想起
你的手会握在别人的手里
你接受别人的爱情
是我熟悉的样子……

Don't make me lose

Don't make me recall

Your hands were being held by another

You accepted the love of others

I know this only too well …

1988年

交谈：自言自语

1
仅仅只是心境相同
我们才坐在一起
坐在太阳底下
就这么成了朋友

其实我们知道
相通和理解只是一种愿望
我们会各自走开
留下石头
和阳光

其实朋友就是这么回事
其实都有自己的心事

Conversation: Talking with One's Self

1

Simply because we shared the same mood

We sat together

Under the sun

And became friends

Actually we knew

Mutual understanding was our only wish

We would go our own ways

Leaving stones and sunshine

Behind us

Actually this is how friends are

Actually they have different thoughts

只是在心境相同的时候
我们坐在一起
我们都很真诚
然后我们走开

2
生不过是一件偶然的事情
而活着不容易
尽管我们的生命
不会太长
尽管走这么一趟
也用不了多少日子

想想这个
就少些生气
少些摧残
少些消耗
可我们还是
办不到

3
站到最后

Only when we share the same mood

Do we sit together

We are all sincere

And then we part

2

Life is something accidental

It is not easy to live

Although our lives

May not be too long

Although this journey

Covers not too many days

Just think of this

Lose your temper less often

Torture one another less

Expend less power

However, we cannot achieve this

3

Standing to the last

街道就会冷清

你走回家去

你就会看见

妻子在房间里走动

家具挨着墙壁

左边是台灯

右边是眠床

你就会感到

这一切都很真实

这一切有些荒诞

你和它们只是偶然相遇

组成了某种关系

其实这里边没有欺骗

其实都是本来的样子

其实我们对这个世界存有奢望

其实这就是我们痛苦的根源

4

我们总是陷进去

陷进去就狂热

就痴迷

The street will become desolate

When you return home

You can see

You wife is walking around indoors

The furniture stands against the walls

The desklamp is on the left

The bed is on the right

You will feel

Everything is authentic

Everything is absurd

You just ran into them accidentally

And formed a certain relation with each

Actually there is no deception here

Actually this is the original situation

Actually we have too many hopes for the world

Actually this is the root of our sorrow

4

We always take the plunge

And then become enthusiastic

Become lost

就温情脉脉
然后我们叫喊
然后流血

其实想想
不陷进去又能怎样

5
我们所有的区别
仅仅是我们的名字
甚至声音
甚至纽扣
甚至做爱的时间
和地点

我们总是容忍我们自己
我们总是在牢骚之后
彼此笑笑
我们步调一致
上班或者回家
做各自的事情
我们用同一种方式

Full of tenderness

And then we scream

And then we bleed

Actually, just think of it

What it would be if we didn't take the plunge

5

The collective difference between us

Is to be found in our names

In our sound

In our buttons

In the time and place

We make love

We always tolerate ourselves

We always smile at each other

After we're done with complaining

We have the same pace

When we go to work or return home

Going about our personal business

We use the same method

处理我们的前途

家庭，子女

和我们的爱情

6

今天是节日

节日使所有的中国人

都变得丰富起来

他们都坐在家里

和亲人们交谈

吃好吃的东西

贫穷者一夜间富裕了许多

脸上放着光彩

节日里找不到可心的朋友

节日是一只笼子

所有的中国人都钻进去

显得理所当然

我们不能例外

我们不想孤独

我们就钻进去

在祖宗的牌位下

Deal with our future

Family and children

As well as our love

6

Today is a festival

The festival all the Chinese

Find riches and abundance

They all sit at home

Conversing with loved ones

Enjoying fine food

The poor became rich overnight

Their faces shine incandescently

You cannot find bosom friends during the festival

The festival is a cage

All the Chinese crawl inside

We are no exception

We don't wish to be lonely

So we crawl inside

Under our ancestral tablet

We find all the Chinese

找出所有的中国人
在这一天都说的话题

7
我们想了许多办法
肯定我们的存在
到头来还是发现
我们所做的一切
仅仅是一种努力
白天我们淹没在大街上
晚上我们埋在房子里
闭上眼睛
整个世界都是我们的
睁开眼睛
连我们也是人家的

在生和死之间
我们无法选择
也无法超越
我们活着
然后死去
带不走一根柴火

Share the same topic on this same day

7

We've thought out so many ways

To verify our existence

But at the end of it we discover

Everything we have done

It's just a trial run

In the daytime we were drowned on the streets

In the evening we were buried in our rooms

When we close our eyes

The entire world belongs to us

When we open our eyes

Even we belong to others

Between life and death

We have no choice

We cannot surpass

We live

And then die

Bringing with us not a single matchstick

8
我们制作镣铐
然后我们戴上
我们跳舞
用各种各样的姿势
这是一种状态
一种方式
让我们哭笑不得

就这么我们体验生命
就这么我们以为
我们有了某种意义
并为此泪流满面

9
不知道临死的那一刻
我们歪过头来
会想些什么
我们经历的一切都很具体
包括痛苦
包括欢乐

8

We fashion handcuffs

And then wear them

We dance

In various styles

This is only one state

And one style

We find it both funny and amusing

In this way we experience life

In this way we think

There is a certain significance to it

This is why our faces are swamped in tears

9

We do not know at the moment of death

When we turn around our heads

What will be on our minds

All of the things we experienced were concrete

Including pain

Including joy

而语言和文字
只是一种简单的概括

我们不会太久
我们只有一次
我们继承的是一场绝望的战争
这就是我们全部的光荣
和悲哀

10
我们总是忽略
我们手里的东西
我们想得到更好的
我们总忘不了
我们是人我们了不起
我们遇到的每一件事情
都深奥无比
我们留恋过去向往未来
我们奋斗一生
到头来还是不知道
什么是我们想要的

But language and words

Are only facile summaries

We won't last long

Only once over

We have inherited a dwindling wall

This is all our glory

And sadness

10

We always neglect

What we hold in our hands

We want something better

We are never able to forget

We are human beings and so great

Everything we run into

Is too inscrutable

We linger in the past and yet look ahead

We struggle all our lives

Until in the end we do not know

What we really wanted

其实我们比兔子还蠢

不吃窝边草

而远处的又吃不到

11

在院子里我们

设计流浪的方案

我们把虚幻的经历

想得悲惨又悲惨

然后我们怜惜自己

为自己感动

就这么我们画地为牢异想天开

就这么我们丰富了一会儿

伟大了一会儿

然后像饺子一样

掉进锅里

煮成别无二致的表情

12

我们和苍蝇作战

我们埋怨冷天气

Actually we are stupider than rabbits

We do not eat the grass from around our nest

But are incapable of eating grass from far away

11

In our courtyard

We plan our wanderings

We think out imaginary experiences

More wretched and miserable

That we take pity on ourselves

Moved by ourselves

In this way we draw our prison and fantasize

For a while we are enriched

For a while we are great

Then like a dumpling

We are dropped into the wok

Bearing the same expression as others

12

We fight with flies

We complain the weather is cold

想起来这还是幸运的事情

事实上我们看不见对手

我们只有难受

在这种境地里

也仅仅只有难受

死不了的时候嫌活得太累

真死的时候才知道我们

对什么都有留恋

也许最大的错误就在于

我们不知道真正的对手

正是我们自己

13
超越的企图使我们永不安宁

我们发明思想

想天下事

为情人流泪

我们翻新一些名词和概念

然后我们激动

其实我们没有力量

Actually this is fortuitous

Actually we cannot see our rivals

We have become more sad

In such a climate

We can only be sad

We bemoan how tiring life is when we cannot die

But the moment we die only then do we know

And cannot tear ourselves away from everything

Perhaps our greatest mistake lies in

Knowing our true rival

Is the self

13

Trying to surpass makes us ever restless

We invent thoughts

Thinking of everything under the sun

Shedding tears for our lovers

We make pioneer certain definitions and ideas

And then grow so excited

Actually we are impotent

变成另一种模样

就这么我们伸长脖子

绳索越来越多

白天和睡梦里

都吊在树上

14

钟声响了

我们抬起头

听见有鞭炮声传来

心里就有些激动

谁也没有说话

就这么心里有些激动

这是另一种程式

我们都很熟练

我们毫不费力

就那么我们激动了一下

忽略了最后一声的时辰

是结束还是开始

Turned into another countenance

In this way we crane our necks

We wear more and more lassos

In the day and in our dreams

We are lynched from a tree

14

The bells tolls

We raise our heads

We hear the din of firecrackers

Become excited in our minds

But nobody says anything

The excitement is just in our hearts

This is another formula

We are all familiar with

It cost us nothing

We simply excite ourselves

And overlook the last toll of the bell

Not knowing whether it signifies the beginning or end

15

我们不知道会遇上什么
过来的一切也未必清楚
我们先是孩子
然后是少年
然后一天天长大
无数的人和我们一起生活
想起来还算有些缘分
尽管扳扳指头
能打招呼的也数不出几个

我们同行我们无法交流
这是我们留给生命过程
仅有的遗憾
我们缄默不语
我们的脚步
是这个世界唯一的声音

15

We do not know what we will encounter

Nor are we clear about things past

We were kids to begin with

Then adolescents

And grew up day-by-day

Countless people cohabit with us

Brought together by certain fate

However, counting on our fingers

There are few we can say "hello" to

We travel together but cannot communicate

What we have left of the journey of life

The only regrets

We keep silent

Our footsteps

Are the only sound in the world

2007年

落 叶

一叶知秋
一叶知世界

是秋天的经络
纵横交错的江河
在你的身体里突然凝结

是秋天的日记
曾经喧闹的青春
和美丽的季节挥手告别

是秋天的声响
注定要来的凋谢
对大地的最后一次抚摸

Fallen Leaves

To see the autumn through a leaf
To see the world through a leaf

The texture of the autumn
Is the crossing rivers and seas
Suddenly congealed inside the body

The diary of the autumn
And the once-boisterous youth
Wave farewell to the beautiful season

The sound of the autumn
And the predestined withering
Stroke the earth for the final time

每一片落叶都有日光的颜色
每一片落叶都有月光的颜色
每一片落叶都有风霜的颜色
每一片落叶都是自然的孩子
每一片落叶都是时间的杰作
都是无法书写的生命故事
无言的诉说……

一叶知秋
一叶知世界

Every fallen leaf has the colour of the sunshine

Every fallen leaf has the colour of the moonlight

Every fallen leaf has the colour of life's hardships

Every fallen leaf is a child of nature

Every fallen leaf is a masterpiece of time

All are life stories indescribable in words

And are tales unspoken ...

To see the autumn through a leaf

To see the world through a leaf